Nightmare on Silent Avenue

Chris Green

Lock Down Publications and Ca$h Presents
Nightmare on Silent Avenue

A Novel by *Chris Green*

Chris Green

Lock Down Publications
P.O. Box 944
Stockbridge, Ga 30281

Visit our website @
www.lockdownpublications.com

Lock Down Publications
Like our page on Facebook: Lock Down Publications @
www.facebook.com/lockdownpublications.ldp
Book interior design by: **Shawn Walker**
Edited by: **Shamika Smith**

Stay Connected with Us!

Text **LOCKDOWN** to 22828 to stay up-to-date with new releases, sneak peaks, contests and more…
Thank you.

Submission Guideline.

Submit the first three chapters of your completed manuscript to ldpsubmissions@gmail.com, subject line: Your book's title. The manuscript must be in a .doc file and sent as an attachment. Document should be in Times New Roman, double spaced and in size 12 font. Also, provide your synopsis and full contact information. If sending multiple submissions, they must each be in a separate email.

Have a story but no way to send it electronically? You can still submit to LDP/Ca$h Presents. Send in the first three chapters, written or typed, of your completed manuscript to:

LDP: Submissions Dept
P.O. Box 944
Stockbridge, Ga 30281

DO NOT send original manuscript. Must be a duplicate.

Provide your synopsis and a cover letter containing your full contact information.

Thanks for considering LDP and Ca$h Presents.

Dedication

This writing thing was never a life that I knew would grasp me so quickly. I've grown to love everything about the art, and it has broadened my visions to bigger heights. I've written a lot of things in my life. Do I have things that you already love? That is a decision for you to decide. Lol. This style of me is different, so I decided to take my journey to another level and try to give you a deeper side of my ambitions. My talk game is amazing, and I've realized that if you don't have any creativity with your flow, it'll hinder you. Be you. Love you. Support you, and everyone else will do as they see. This book is dedicated to my one and only daughter, Massiyah, my mother, Dee-Dee, my brother, Lowski, and all the loving family members I have that have been showing me the most ultimate support. I have loving fans everywhere, and only a few REAL fans will be able to recognize the man behind this mirror. This book is also dedicated to you, but that doesn't mean to go ruin the joy for everyone else and give up my disguise. My name is Shakur Diamond, and I'm gonna stamp my name in this game as one of the best authors who've done it. #LDPMadeMe...

Acknowledgments

I would like to thank the King of Kings. The boss man, Author Ca$h, for a blazing opportunity to be someone in this book world. I remember reading your books in the county ten years ago and shaking my head at how good your novels were. I barely wanted to let another read it in fear that they were gonna bend the cover. Now I'm actually striving for the same company's books that I was just reading to pass my time. Much gratitude for that!

I would like to acknowledge all the ones who at least picked up the phone when I called from these tough prison walls. LisaLuvv...You are an amazing woman. One that I pray to grow closer with and keep by my side for eternity. I'm happy to call you a friend and a Queen with outstanding motivation for a person when things seem to be so down. I love you.

My mother. You've grown with me, and of course, we all have downs, but I've never met a mommy that will not let anything bypass her when it comes to the babies that she birthed. Your love is my push, so please keep it coming, mother. After all, I'm on my way out that door.

As for all my friends who I thought were so-called down for me, thank you, guys, for showing me just how bad I was stuck in that piece of tar. None of you are by my side at this present time, and it all began with at least twelve of us. I watched that number click down slowly until I was left alone with no one but my mother and talent. The exact ones I started with. Still in all, I wish you guys no harm, and it damn sure ain't no bad blood. I'm just glad to say that snakes like y'all can never hurt me again or gain the trust I have within my soul. Thank y'all for making me a better person.

Now that I've spilled my shout-outs, dig into this story of captivating hood secrets that will leave you speechless on *Silent Avenue*. #LDPMadeMe!

Prologue
Melly

December 25, 1996, was a day that I could never forget. We were staying off in this nice ass crib down on Eason Street, 1358, to be exact. This was the westside of Atlanta. A nasty neighborhood to have yo upbringing, and probably where you needed to carry a gun just to keep the tennis shoes that your mama bought you for the new school year.

I had just opened my eyes, staring at the alarm clock on the dresser for the twentieth time. Pops would always go by the same rule every year. Never get up and touch them damn gifts until after six in the morning. The holidays were traditional under our roof. Family would always flood my dad's shit to feast off my mama's finger-licking good food, and everybody damn sure was stepping through to exchange gifts. Being the only child made shit so sweet. I was only six at the time, and even though I didn't have everything I wanted, my mom and pops tried to make sure I was straight by any means. You didn't usually see a nigga's father toting real paper just from working a regular nine-to-five job, but recently my pops had finally received a blessing from the man above to strike the lottery for a nice piece of change. At least that's what he told my mama. The past three months had been so lovely. The new car, the house, the expensive shopping sprees, it really felt like those hard-ass poverty days were over. Still in all, there was never a such thing as a bright day when you lived on the streets of Silent Avenue.

Hearing my mama and auntie gossip in the living room, I jumped out of bed faster than Flash. I was hoping that I had something better than the Scooby-Doo pajamas I had on my ass to wear up under the tree. Even though pops had that spare dough, he was big on not wasting it for miscellaneous shit. If it involved the family household, he was with it. However, some personal materialistic stuff to brag and flaunt was out of the question before you even had the chance to ask for it.

As soon as I reached the family room, my mama's honey-hazel eyes locked in on me with a big smile. "Hey, mama's baby." She held out her arms, wanting her morning hug as usual.

You know me. I was a whole mama's boy for real, and I couldn't help but sprint over by her side and latching my arms around her waist. You can smell the holiday food she was fixing up lingering from her apron as she picked up a yellow box with a red ribbon from under the tree.

"Here, Melly. Open mama's present first." She placed it in my hands, just snickering as if it was the best surprise that I'd ever see.

Rushing to sit my ass down, I placed the box in front of me just as the doorbell rang twice. I was so excited that I kept my attention on the Christmas wrapper I was now shredding to pieces when my aunt Fema headed to answer the door. Opening the box, the first thing I noticed was the shiny Cuban link bracelet that rested on top of an all-black Ralph Lauren sweat suit. My face glowed up like the sun on a Friday morning when I picked it up and read the word "Love" that was engraved on the small clipping.

"Hey! Merry Christmas, family. How y'all living this morning?" I heard a thick voice that caused my head to rise.

My auntie Fema was laughing and hugging this man that was draped down in an all-black two-piece suit. His hair was curly like wool with thick eyebrows, and he chewed on a piece of bubble yum while scanning the room as if he was looking for someone specific. I watched him walk over to my mama, placing a firm kiss on her cheek, while she sat in the new Lay-z-boy chair my dad just brought home the day before.

12

"Wassup, Felicia? Merry Christmas, girl," he mouthed with a sly grin on his face.

My eyes couldn't help but stare at the big green gift box in his hand, wondering who it was for.

"Thanks, boy. You know Franklin had to work, so it's just me, Fema, and Melly until everybody else shows up later on," my mama replied before picking up her copy of the *Atlanta Journal Constitutional* newspaper.

That one statement caused him to pause before his eyes landed on me with a wicked smile. "Damn, that's too bad. I was hoping to catch all of y'all at once." His tone trailed off before I recognized the black handgun he was pulling from his pants.

Boom!

The first bang and flash distorted my hearing and vision for a slight moment. That was the bullet hitting my mama, Felicia, in the head and forcing the newspaper to drop gently from her palms. So much blood was rushing down her face, and all I could make out was Fema screaming at the top of her lungs.

Boom!

The second bullet from his gun ripped through Fema's chest, forcing her at least four feet back until she crashed under the mantelpiece. I could tell that she was dead from the way her bulging eyes glared at me. Even after watching the two closest women to me be slain like runaway slaves, I couldn't fix my body to move an inch. The nigga's eyes rotated back to me with a huge smile like the Grinch himself. The lights from the Christmas tree flickered like a horror scene, and his eyes looked as if they were dilating wider as he stepped closer to me. At that moment, I wanted to cry for my father, but I knew that it would do no good. Kneeling on one knee, he placed the box directly in front of me. The devil's aura could be felt rising off his thick skin as his chest heaved with adrenaline.

"Open it, lil nigga." His tone was exciting but demanding at the same time.

My fingers trembled in fear as I kept my eyes trained on him. Reaching for the top, I removed it slowly and felt the center of my chest cave in like a professional baseball player striking me with a hard swing from his bat. A small salty tear dropped down my cheek, sliding down to the side of my lips, allowing me to taste the pain I actually felt surfacing throughout my body. My dad, Franklin's, severed head looked up at me with torture written all over his face. The pit of my stomach was bubbling harder than a pot of heating vegetable oil when he lifted my chin with a finger and spoke. "All you need is love, and you ain't gotta beg me to help. You're loved. Merry Christmas," he whispered in my ear before rising back to his feet.

A small chuckle escaped his lips as I stared down into the box at what was left of my dad. The killer never showed any emotion for his heartless act. As he walked towards the front door, he turned around to say one last thing. His voice was now drawling out like a demonic spirit. "Wake up, Melly. The nightmare is over. Wake up!"

Jumping up from my sleep, I looked over at my girlfriend, Kay-Kay, shaking my shoulder for me to wake up. Her beautiful round face was close to mines expressing worry, and I could tell by the way she was breathing that I was obviously having another bad dream.

"Wassup Kay?" I sat up on the side of my bed with sweat dripping severely from my forehead.

"You, Melly. I'm starting to worry about you, baby. Your dreams are getting worse, and you're starting to talk in your sleep." She kissed the side of my neck and rubbed my shoulder with empathy.

I didn't wanna speak on the same shit as always, and quite frankly, I was tired of the bad visions that kept replaying in my mind since that disastrous day. Taking my shirt off, I wiped the sweat from my body and tossed it in the clothes hamper. Looking at the clock that read 6:01, I exhaled and rubbed my temples to slightly ease my tension. Turning around, my eyes gazed into Kay-Kay's. Grabbing a handful of her fat and soft booty, I curled under her like a newborn baby. You know I had to kiss one of them titties through her shirt. That shit always made her giggle, and it was the only way I would know she wasn't going to sleep worried about me.

"Stop Melllyyy!" She popped the back of my head playfully.

When I saw that beautiful smile blush across her chunky red cheeks, I began to relax. I started to slowly feel myself drifting back into a deep sleep, this time, praying that my head didn't replay those terrifying moments that scarred me for life.

Chris Green

Chapter 1
Kay-Kay
Martin Luther King Jr. Drive

I was awoken from the sound of Alicia Keys playing smoothly through the speakers in my living room. I could still feel the backache I caught in the middle of the night from dealing with Melly's freaky ass, and the sun was piercing through my side window like a peeping tom with a flashlight. I rolled and stretched around in my bed, realizing that his big head ass had left me to cuddle by myself. That boy knew I was selfish when it came down to being comfortable and feeling like the most cherished woman in the world. Regardless of how much I cursed him for doing the opposite, he would always hit me with that seductive little smile and chuckle like Denzel on *Training Day*. That shit has worked since we were in high school, and it still was able to make my belly turn in circles with butterflies feeling as if they were lifting me off my feet. He was my Hercules, my bundle of ass pain that I wouldn't get rid of for any man in this world.

Getting the energy to stand up, I quickly went into the bathroom to brush my teeth. I couldn't help but hum Alicia's song with her as I squeezed the Close-Up toothpaste in my mouth.

"Some people want it all, but I don't want nothing at all. If it ain't youuuu, babyyy! If I ain't got you babyy. Some people want diamond rings, some just want everythingg, but everything means nothing. If I ain't got you babyy," I hummed and nodded my head with my hand waving around as if I was performing for a fifty-thousand crowd audience on Broadway.

After my small episode of feeling like a star, I let my hair out of the bun allowing it to drop down my back. Once I washed my face, I headed for the living room to see why

Melly was beating R&B early in the morning like he was having an emotional breakdown. When I finally spotted him, he was sweeping the floor in a pair of basketball shorts, no shirt, and a pair of Nike flip-flops. I stood there staring at my cup of chocolate milk as if he were the last nutritious drink on earth. His body was more than fit, from his chest down to the abs, calves, and legs. We usually went to L.A. Fitness at least twice a week to make sure we stayed in shape. Of course, I was forced, and he never wanted me to start on anything else without doing ass squats. "Baby, you gotta keep that shit poking," is what he would say before we could even get through the doors good.

His eyes finally looked up, catching me in deep thought as I stared him down. His pupils scanned up my body. I could see him gazing at the tight lace boyshort panties hugging my big booty. My little Star Wars T-shirt he won from the last year's carnival was his favorite, and of course, I had my pretty toes out. They would always curl up on the side from the cold floor whenever I stood somewhere too long, like at that exact moment.

"You must want me to eat that right now, instead of the breakfast I made?" he asked, making his chest jump like those buff supermodels on the workout channel.

I pouted my lips, placing my little red hand over my crotch with a naughty nod. When he dropped the broom moving towards me, I cried in laughter. "Nooo, Melly. I'm just playing, bay. You did enough last night, freaky man." I held my hands out in front of me in surrender.

That nigga didn't know how to act in the cooch, and I had to be at work in the next hour. So, playing around with Mr. Tube Sock, as he called it, was out of the question. "Why are you up so early in yo sexy man mood?" I pecked his lips twice, not wanting to stop his cleaning mode.

18

"It was kinda hard for me to sleep last night, Kay. Those dreams are like little crab bugs jumping on a dirty bitch." He scratched his chest, making me laugh at his stupid self.

"Boy, you been having those same dreams since we were in high school. A dirty girl ain't got nothing to do with it. You scared me this time, Melly. You were calling your dad's name and you ain't gotta beg me to help. You're loved."

Chris Green

Chapter 2
Bleeko

As I pulled up in front of Melly's crib, I couldn't help but to drop my top down on the new 2018 Lexus GX460. I was so much of a graceful nigga that I only received the best of the best blessings from the man they claimed to be above us. Checking out my handsome face in the rear-view mirror, I honked the horn twice and stepped out. Even though I was a short nigga, I never moved around my hood like I wasn't the biggest motherfucker on the block. I kept my hair smoother than a nigga on a jar of Murray's hair grease and always dressed in the best designer shit that dropped. My brown stitched Fendi jacket matched the pockets on my bleached Salvatore Ferragamo jeans. Of course, my T-shirt was fitted with the large double F symbol glossing like the label was laminated on the smooth polyester. I was truly the meaning of fresh to death because every bitch I ditched back then tried their best to kill me when their eyes landed on this playa. I was thirty years old and ain't never had shit when I was younger. Now that I was older with a bankroll bigger than the slave masters these cats in the hood were working for, I showed my ass on a 24/7 basis. I sacrificed and put everything on the line to earn my name on Silent Avenue, and now I was gonna show motherfuckers the reason they all were gonna be screaming the name Bleeko until the end of time.

Hearing my young nigga, Melly, step out of his ole lady's front door, I flashed a huge grin throwing my hands up in the air. I never met a young cat like him with a mean hustle game, and I had to tip my hat to the young nigga. If provoked, he could be a disaster to someone's life. I met him at the age of five through his father, Franklin, the same man who was my mentor. Unfortunately, he got mixed in some sticky shit which ended up with half of their family getting whacked. It was a sad moment for any young cat who was molded by the vet, but in the end, we couldn't speak on shit like that when you were from the neighborhood where we grew up in.

"Damn nigga. How many cars you gonna buy around this bitch?" Melly asked me while rubbing his hands across the caramel leather of my passenger seat. He didn't waste any time jumping inside going straight for a nigga's radio system as always.

I nodded, giving him the okay to crank that bitch to the max. Once the Tupac song, *Hail Mary,* started to blast through the speakers, his entire posture changed. His fingers were stuck on the dial as if he just froze in fucking time. I didn't know if it was the Alpine speakers knocking a hole through his head or if he just deleted his ear drum for a second. Snapping my fingers repeatedly, he jumped out of his daydream and quickly turned the volume down.

"You alright?" I asked, looking down at him with a curious eye.

"Yeah… Hell yeah, man. I just was zoned out thinking 'bout some other shit. My bad." He nodded, but he didn't seem too sure from the look on his face.

"You sure?"

"Yeah, nigga. I'm positive."

Taking his word for it, I jumped in the driver's seat and swerved off with my tires hollering off the concrete. I dug in my middle console grabbing the rolled Dutch Master full of Kush, and sparked it. Taking a few pulls, I tried to pass it to Melly's nonsmoking ass.

"Come on, man. Stop playing, Bleek!" He quickly pushed it back towards me as if that shit were poisonous venom from a rattlesnake's mouth.

I couldn't help but laugh at the young nigga. He was like a Christian kid. The nigga didn't smoke, drink, cheat, or even too tough to carry a weapon. It was a surprise to see how many people who actually feared him and gave respect throughout the streets we played on. "What's up with you and this drug-free ass life, my nigga? You don't wanna drink no lean wit ya big brother or smoke a joint. God damn nigga, Kay-Kay got that act right coochie, don't it?" I laughed before busting a left down on Simpson and Chappell.

"Nah, man. You know that shit ain't my style. Drugs pollute the mind, bro. I'm already doing enough hustling on these busted-ass streets. I'm ready to break free, man, and I damn sho can't do that living in the hype with all this temptation floating around me." He looked at me with a straight face.

"Mannn… Nigga this is Atlanta. You see me, baby boy. I pop bottles, fuck any bitch I want, get money, and still can handle whatever drug I decide to party on for the day. Don't get it twisted, Melly. This shit only crumbles the lame-ass hustlers who were never meant to be in a position from the jump. If a man makes an excuse for being broke and not living life to the fullest, he's suffering from one or two things. Being scared of living free or waiting for a handout off another man," I said before stepping out of the car. "You need somethin' out the store?"

"Yeah, man. A Lipton iced tea."

"See, that shit right there sounds extra gay." I laughed and headed for the entrance before he could throw the empty soda can towards me.

Strolling inside the Hunter Hills Food Market, I made my way to the drink section, snatching lil bro and me up something to sip on. I laid eyes on the nigga Lonnie when I walked through the door, and he was so busy entertaining that rotten ass hoe, Latoya, that he ain't never see me slide through the entrance quicker than a dick up a supermodel's ass. The bitch nigga had been owing me two thousand dollars for the past month but was ducking me every time I would slide down his way. It was always an excuse when I ran into his brother, but today was cash-in day, and I wasn't agreeing to anything different. The store was small, so after I let the last few customers clear out, I slowly pushed up the center aisle on a mission. By the time he noticed me walking up on his register, I pushed the slut bucket, Latoya, with a nasty look on my face, and ice grilled his dumb ass. "What the fuck up with it, Lonnie? I been having my eye out for my check and still ain't seen that shit like you promised me last month, fool."

I can see the pussy ready to form where this nigga's nuts were supposed to hang at because he was fidgeting like his bitch ass had an audition for *American Idol*.

"Bleeko, bruh, I was just talking to my brother, trying to get yo number from him, man. I found a little hook-up on some work, right? They fronted me a little zip of clean, so I should be able to run that up for you in another few weeks," he said as if that shit was cool without asking me.

I tapped my fingers gently against the register, wondering if he was gonna bust out and tell me that he was just bullshitting, and the bread was really in his pockets. I noticed after I was quiet for a few seconds too long. He sat back on the railing of the counter, with his arms folded as if there was nothing else to speak on. I kept my eyes trained on this idiot while waving towards Latoya to get the fuck out of the store. After the bell on the door sounded off, indicating that she followed my orders, I pulled out my 9mm Beretta, placing one in the chamber.

"I'm not sure if you heard me, Lonnie. I need my money now. Not in a couple of weeks, lil nigga. My patience has been cut thinner than those punk-ass braids in ya head. If I wait any longer, you're gonna be bald, and I'll be broke," I said humbly, hoping that he got the picture.

I watched his eyes rotate down to my strap and back up at me with a smirk. "If you kill me, how the fuck I'ma pay you, dumb-dumb? I think it's best if you just have patience. You know who my brother is, Bleeko," he said with emphasis like I gave a fuck.

I remained calm but started to get the memo that he was clearly saying my paper was a dead issue. Aiming my strap to his right eye, I pulled the trigger before his bitch ass could utter another word.

Boc!

I watched his brains spray from the back of his head like a Febreze bottle before he crumbled behind the counter. Making sure I ended the debt for sure, I moved around to where his body laid stiffly and placed two more hot ones in his chest.

Boc! Boc!

"Fuck nigga!" I mumbled before tucking my pistol and heading for the door. Flipping the open sign to closed, I stepped out of the store with the drinks in my left hand and quickly got in the car. Melly was looking at me with a crazy expression before hitting me with a dumb-ass question.

"Were those gunshots I just heard?"

Handing him the tea, I cranked my whip with a dumb ass face before pulling off. "Naw, the nigga in the store was popping them dumb ass firecrackers like he stupid. I almost popped his ass thinking somebody was trying to get at me."

Melly shook his head with a smile as I flushed the coupe down Silent Avenue and turned down West Lake. My eyes stayed on the rearview mirror until I reached the expressway down by the train station. I didn't hesitate to jump on that motherfucker doing the dash to let the hood cool down for a sec. The one thing I wasn't tolerating was disrespect when I showed love to the people. I refused to be a product by allowing niggas to buck on my product. It was either gonna be correct business or the best exchange for whatever a nigga owed. That's just the way I got down.

* * *

Greenbriar Mall
Cutz and Styles Barbershop
Melly

After making our way across town to the Zone Four area, Bleeko decided to stop at the Cutz Barbershop in the mall. It was a normal hangout for the city niggas to chill in, and half of Atlanta made their way inside to get a trim up from one of the best barbers in the shop, Tee.

Walking through the entrance doors of the grooming spot, Mr. Randy and Trouble Man's eyes landed on me immediately. These old head niggas had been giving me hell since I was a little boy coming in the shop with my dad. They knew Franklin for two things: getting money and getting away with murder. Still, it didn't stop their old asses from putting the major press on me to see if I had my daddy's bones soaking in my body.

"Melly Mel. Wassup lil man?" Randy raised his hand while sitting down in the empty barber chair.

"What's good, Randy? What up, Trouble Man?" I smiled, grabbing one of the open seats.

Bleeko didn't waste any time heading over to Tee's chair after watching a customer get up. He didn't give a damn that he just jumped the line on the two other young dudes that were waiting patiently before we even arrived.

"Boy, you don't even come to kick it with the old crew no more. I think the last time I cut yo hair, you was going on a field trip to the Coca-Cola factory in the third grade." Randy laughed, showing all his crooked buttery teeth.

He was an ugly mother-shut-yo-mouth, and all his clothes smelt like that cheap ass black suede cologne they used to sell in front of all the thrift stores. The one thing I knew about Mr. Randy and Trouble Man was that they loved to get them some paper and trick off on some fine-ass women. That's been their motto since I was a child. You weren't talking 'bout shit if you ain't never paid for no tricks. It was funny to me because I know these fools were dead ass serious. "Man, shut up, Randy. I just came and spent some money with you last month."

He looked off in the sky with a dumb-ass gaze as if he was trying to remember. "You damn sho right, son. That's the twenty dollars I gave freak number seven hundred and twenty-eight!" He and Trouble Man shared a laugh and a high five.

You know I couldn't help but laugh at his mental health ass, especially when a bad sister walked in the door with her young son beside her. "Hey, Tee. I'm gonna let him wait here while I do a little shopping. Clean him up for me?" she spoke with a sexy ass tone.

Tee nodded with a smile and continued to cut on Bleeko's head.

"Well, I'll be damned, sister. Tee ain't the only handsome ass brother in this shop, baby girl. They say I make women crave Mayfield ice cream and Cheeto Puffs after getting some good loving from me. Who gave you all that stuffing back there in yo muffin?" Randy grumbled like he was eating a piece of good chicken.

Her gorgeous face was definitely immaculate, from the hot pink lips to her ambiguous colored eyes. She sported a Calvin Klein women's sweat suit, along with a pair of diamond-studded hoop earrings. Her hair was dyed blonde and curled freely down to her neck. From the caramel skin down to her hypnotic body said that she was a trophy to some dude, and it was guaranteed that he was probably a killer. I watched her toot her nose up at Randy as if he were a piece of dog shit before walking out.

"You just need to hear some Patti LaBelle and get a good bubble bath with a good one, darling. I'll still be sniffing that ass when you come back to pick up the little one." He tried his best to follow her butt while she walked out of the shop with that thang bouncing from left to right.

"I thank that means she straight on tricking old men. Everybody ain't going for all that weak-ass game." I sat back in my chair, laughing harder than a motherfucka.

Randy pulled a pair of dice from his shirt pocket, shaking them lightly in his balled-up hand. "See, that's the problem with y'all hating ass young niggas. You grew up with little things to offer to these big fine-ass women. You gotta let the grand masters handle all those heavy loads, son. All that ass woulda broke yo little fingers if she decided to drop it in ya lap. I'm talking 'bout just fall right on off ya lil hand. Speaking on grand, what them hustling pockets looking like, chump? Let me show ya how I use to break ole Franklin over here in the cut." He flexed on me, pulling out a wad full of twenty-dollar bills.

Knowing that gambling was a trait I tried to cut back on, I glanced over at Bleeko, who nodded with approval. "I usually don't do this, but I'ma go ahead and break you before I spend a twenty to get my haircut," I said, walking over to the corner. Trouble Man followed, knowing that Randy and I went full throttle when it was a dice game in effect. Watching the old man shoot for the first point, it landed on a four and two. I tossed down a twenty, and before I could even get my leg down on the ground good, he was bringing that shit back, making me drop another dub on the floor. After a few rounds, I realized I had to hold dice on this man. If you didn't stop Randy while he was in full strike mode, ya ass would probably be walking out of his shop with the lint that was in your pocket when you first bought ya jeans out of the store.

"Hold them." I stopped the dice with my hands just when he was about to bust me for another Jackson.

"Damn, nephew. You gotta get that hating ass blood out ya system." He started flipping quickly through the three twenties he took from me like they added up to a cool thousand.

I ignored his ass because I know he was the master of distraction when it came down to getting his bread took. My first strike, I busted the number seven and picked up my dub.

"Put down." I flexed, dropping forty on the floor.

"Come on, baby boy. That ain't nothing, but coochie fare." He bet against me.

No hesitation, I rolled the dice cracking his ass with a five and two, picking my money up the smooth way. That shit hyped me up, and fifteen minutes later, I found myself sweating in the corner with a whole new crowd of niggas behind us watching the heated ass gambling pot. Randy had come out of his barber shirt to try and get back with all the bread that I was snatching out of his slacks. I hadn't put the dice down once since my last crap out, and now I was up four thousand dollars on his dumb ass. I cut my eyes, noticing the last hundred-dollar bill he was clutching on to for dear life. The entire barbershop was whispering, knowing if Randy got those dice back, he was gonna try to show his ass. That was the last thing on my mind because I wasn't tryna see that happen. Counting out five twenties, I dropped them on the floor. "Bet all that shit, cap ass old man!"

I could tell he was mad as fuck. His eyes were cocked like a pistol, and he kept licking his dry ass lips, looking back and forth at the floor like some cash was gonna reappear back on the ground. I cheered with joy in my mind when he bit the bait, dropping his last hundo. "You ain't no real dice shooter like Franklin. Bet!"

I smiled hearing that bullshit. I was my dad's exact image, and my confidence was more than high when I was tested on that. Kissing his dice, I tossed them bitches across the wall, watching my seven smack against the floor like a magnet had grabbed ahold of them. A smile crept across my face when everybody behind me started to shout with laughter from Randy's boo-boo face. Bleeko was just climbing out of the chair, shaking his head, knowing I was the truth. He watched Randy standing with a hand on his chin, rubbing it like he was waiting for something to grow. Rising up, I grabbed the hundred-dollar bill, slapping it back in his palm. "That's for my next five haircuts, Jive Turkey-ass old man. I should make you give me a shoeshine for bending down so long." I chuckled, counting through the quick flip I made.

"Nigga, I got fillings in my mouth older than you. That shit ain't do nothing but made me hungry for some more paper, baby." He stuffed the money in his pants and pointed at all the freeloading brothers who were posted in his shop. "If y'all broke Church's Chicken eating-ass leaches ain't spending no loot on a cut, bounce ya ass out my establishment like a Juvenile video. Let's go." Randy waved his hands towards the door.

Bleeko and I shared a laugh as we pushed off with the crowd. The fine Sista who dropped off her son earlier was standing by the soda machine with a smile touching both of her cheeks. She didn't utter a word when I moved past her as she placed a piece of paper in my hand with a wink.

Opening it up, I looked at the phone number and the words "TEXT ME" were in bold letters. Smirking, I glanced back at her sliding it inside of my pocket.

"Damn Casanova. You coulda let me catch that lil nookie. You ain't bout to do nothing with that." Bleeko rubbed a hand through his head, blowing the chick a kiss through the glass.

Instead of replying, I remained quiet. He was right about one thing. I damn sure wasn't about to do shit with her, but that doesn't mean he was good enough to have the sweetheart who offered me the number. Kay-Kay was my Queen, and there was nothing another woman could offer to make me cheat or leave her side. Still, it didn't give me the right to offer baby girl's info to a nigga she didn't wanna give it to. Certain females just needed direction with the men they chose, and even though I wasn't the right one, it didn't mean that I would lead her to a fool's arms who was surely gonna be wrong. "She might just be a friend," I replied just to kill all hopes of him asking me anything stupid.

"Yeah, a friend," he mumbled, glancing at his watch. "I know you gotta nice lil piece of change in ya pockets, so I'm pushing over to a few of my spots to pick up some cookies of that dope to take back to Silent Avenue with us."

"Say less. I probably have a few hours to make my quota on the block before Kay-Kay gets off anyway. I can spare some time."

"Bet."

As we walked out of the Greenbriar Mall, I pictured the smile of the woman who just placed her number in my hand. I wanted to just ball it up and toss it on the ground, but something in my heart said to do the opposite. Bleeko jumped on his phone before we reached the car. Once I climbed into the passenger seat, I took the battery out of my phone and put the number underneath it before placing it back together. That day was also one that I would never forget. One that would be a life-or-death situation in my future.

Chapter 3
West End, Avon Avenue, and Lorenzo Drive
Melly

Pulling up to the house where Bleeko laid his head, we cut the loud ass music off and hopped out of the car. A few niggas occupied the yard playing a hand of spades at a rusty wooden table. I could see the big ass guns they had sitting underneath that motherfucker for a nigga who thought shit was sweet. Bleeko was a wild head, but he was smart. He had money, so paying niggas to do his dirty work was an easy way to make his day flow even smoother unless it was just that personal.

"Y'all retards better make sure APD don't pull up on my damn porch with all of them guns out like that, man," he mentioned to the four men before we walked in the house.

"Man, shut yo scary-ass up," I heard one of them reply before I could close the door behind us.

I had to laugh because Bleeko just kept it pushing like he was the President in that bitch. His crib was better than tight. Two seventy-inch flat screens were mounted around his living room. One with a game system, the other playing a loud ass FX movie on surround sound speakers. A large fish tank was glowing up on the far-left wall. I couldn't help but push up, staring at all the exotic fish swimming around inside.

"Make ya self at home, lil brudda. My shit, yo shit." Bleeko sparked up a blunt that sat on an oval-shaped glass table. A few kids ran from the back, hugging his legs as if they were the happiest babies in the world. They couldn't have been no older than five and six.

"Heyyy Uncle Bleekk," their voices yelled out in unison.

"Wassup bad assses? Why y'all ain't outside somewhere playing, and which one of y'all smell like piss?" he asked, smelling their clothes one by one. "Go and get in the tub, man.

All y'all. I'ma send ya mama to get some Mickey Ds in a second."

You could hear the joy in their tones as they broke, running for the back of their home like a small football team. A few women moved around the house talking on phones and talking loud as shit. I just sat back on the couch and started to engage in the *Madden 2020* game that was on pause. Bleeko made his way into the kitchen that sat behind me, so I already knew that it was probably time for him to cook up a batch of the strong pack. The cocaine he was plugged in on was more than raw. That shit was toxic. I had been dealing with him since I was seventeen, and from my knowledge, he never was caught with any bullshit dope. The name Big Sal always roamed around, but no one was able to say they've ever seen the nigga. Bleeko was his trusted business partner, but every time I asked him to meet the man, he just brushed it off and told me the same shit. "Nobody wants to meet Sal. Just leave that to me and make the money, kiddo." I took that as he was obviously cautious on who he dealt with, so I just sat back and got in where I fitted.

My attention was quickly taken when I noticed someone out the corner of my eye standing to the side of me. I paused the game, and my eyes rotated over to a tall, chocolate woman who wore nothing but a pair of thin black tights and a black sports bra. Her hair was in long micro braids that stopped at the center of her back. I had to swallow my spit from how hard she was gazing me up and down. Moving over to the TV in front of me, she bent over, reaching down under the entertainment center for a fresh cigarillo. Her ass was bigger than any woman I've ever been around. I mean, a true stallion. This girl clearly didn't have on any panties from the way her shit jiggled around freely, and I could tell she was taking her time by the way she arched her back. I made sure to look away until she grabbed all the damn blunts that she needed. When she walked back over to the couch, sitting beside me, my heartbeat sped up.

"Hey, boy. What's yo name?"

"Melly." I kept my eyes trained on the game, feeling her eyes molest me.

"Melly, huh?"

"Yeah."

I could see her quickly rolling the blunt as if she were on a mission. She pearled it to perfection and used the lighter on the table to spark it. Her ass still didn't move, which forced me to look over at her. I could smell some good ass perfume creeping from underneath her clothes, and a few pieces of nice gold jewelry was on her body. Her large black lips inhaled the weed, and she matched my stare as if she was ready to shoot it out.

"You fine as a motherfucker, Melly. You wanna fuck?" she asked bluntly as if I didn't just meet her forty-six seconds ago.

I was so shocked that I had to scratch my head and make sure I wasn't tripping. "Huh?" I uttered as if I didn't hear what she offered the first time.

"I said do you wanna fuck, nigga?" she asked louder.

"Uhh, nah. I'm good. Thanks." I tried to get back on the game like that shit didn't just throw my mind for a full loop. Bleeko had some true gangsta ass bitches in his crib if they were moving direct like the one next to me, and I didn't even know who the fuck she was. I was praying that nigga walked out of the kitchen so I wouldn't be the one getting mixed in the blender if it happened to be his lil side chick or some shit.

I guess this bitch felt like my answer wasn't good enough because she reached over, grabbing a handful of my dick as if it didn't belong to me. She even squeezed it to make sure it was there.

"And yo shit big. I'll suck the skin off that bitch," she laughed.

Pushing her hand off me, I scooted slightly over with a stupid ass look on my face. I watched her get up and clap her ass as if she were auditioning for a porn video. "My room is the one to the far back, on the left. Don't leave here without pulling up Melly. With yo black, cute, big dick ass." She walked off like she didn't just rob me for a free grabby.

After she disappeared around the corner, I got my ass up faster than a bolt of lightning and headed for the kitchen. Bleeko was standing over the stove with a glass Pyrex in hand, and his phone was up to his ear. I sat at the kitchen table looking at the four bricks he had out like the shit was just legal. I wasn't going back in the living room where the pickle monster just left, so I took a seat and waited patiently until Bleek ended his call.

"Aye. I need you to grab six of those plastic Ziplocs and bag up an ounce for me. It's almost time to head over to Cleveland before we take it home." He looked back at me, trying his best not to fuck up on his whipping process.

"I got you, man."

I grabbed the scale from the top of his refrigerator and quickly weighed up twenty-eight grams of the strong ass dope he had sitting on the table. Being careful not to hold that shit in between my fingers too long, I double bagged it and washed my hands with a little bit of the dish liquid the was by the sink.

Bleeko didn't take long to wrap up at the stove, but I guess he kinda peeped my facial expression before I could allow myself to let the recent situation in his living room fade from my head.

"Nigga, you aite? Why ya looking like you lost ya best friend?"

Embarrassed to explain what occurred, I just asked a simple question. "Who's the tall, dark skin chick with the braids?"

Bleeko thought for a few seconds before answering, "Ohh, you talking 'bout my sister, Fanta's crazy ass. That's my mama's daughter. Why?"

"Man, she got press like a nigga." I shook my head.

Bleeko just laughed before placing the Pyrex in the sink. "She just tried to trick you in that room, didn't it?"

"How you know?"

"Cause nigga. She's my sister. That girl is freakier than a Rick James and Prince concert, but she ain't trying you unless she likes ya. She's rarely down here in the A, but when she is, somebody gonna get snatched up by her mental health ass. Don't go for it. Sis be having them niggas going crazy, but she's dangerous."

"Shit, I already feel like she snatched me up. She just tries and takes what she wants, I see." I handed Bleeko the packaged dope.

"Yeah, she'll get down if you don't stop her." He tossed me the car keys before walking down the hallway that led to their bedrooms.

By the time he was making his way back to the front, his sister, Fanta, was directly behind him. Her eyes locked in on me like a pit spotting a kid on an early school morning. "Melly, why you telling my brother on me? I'ma still fuck you, boy." She giggled like that shit was a threat.

That was the first time I can say I ran because I wasted no time getting my ass up out that front door. Fanta would be the type of chick that got a nigga in some grave trouble, and I didn't even wanna get my mind intertwined with nothing her big thick self had going on. By the time she reached the doorway, I was waving bye and hopping in the passenger seat of Bleeko's Lexus.

Pulling my phone out, I checked the notifications and spotted a message from Kay-Kay.

Kaycake: Hey Zaddyyyy. I hope you're doing something productive and negative free my King. I don't get off until 9:30. Would you like me to pick you up something to eat?

Me: Wassup my love... I'm always doing something with my time. Positivity brings prosperity bay. I would like some Wendy's and a side order of some Kay coochie salad. Lol!

It didn't take long for me to receive a reply after sending my message.

Kaycake: Mmmhmm. I got you baby. Those tiny ass Wendy's burgers can't fill you up like a Kay coochie salad. I'll be naked before I get out of the car with my bottle of ranch in hand. I'm about to tell my boss to relieve me right now. Cook me up some meat to go inside my lettuce. Lol.

Me: You better not leave them little kids' mouths like that. They need their dentist to stay focused. I'll have your meal prepared by the time you reach home. I promise.

Bleeko climbing in the front seat forced me to look up and make sure Big Fanta wasn't about to try and rape some shit. I didn't have time to wrestle with all that because she damn sho was gonna win.

"Boy, I don't know what the hell you did to my sister, but she was trying to pay me to bring you back over here."

"Hell nah. Yo sister will fuck around and make my wife leave me," I laughed, thinking about how good all that ass would feel getting thrown back against me. Once I realized that Kay-Kay was past mental and threatened me that if I ever gave her dick away, she was gonna cut me up and put my ass on the grill, I quickly tossed that shit out of my mind. Her red ass was enough for me, and that pussy was sweeter than any fruit I'd had in my life. All the tension I had built up at that moment, her ass was probably gonna get bent into a pretzel by the time I got ahold of that cookie. It was even funnier because her message came back through before I could turn the music up to Bleeko's radio as he pulled out of the parking lot.

Kaycake: You better not be doing nothing I wouldn't be doing, or I'll be out shopping for a grill tomorrow. Lol I love you Melly.

That shit made me crack up, and I knew for sure that my baby was a straight lunatic. It was the reason I loved her so much. She kept a nigga grounded on loyalty, and whenever my mind seemed like it was slipping. I always got some good food for thought out of her. She was smart, beyond gorgeous, and the most spoiled woman I could ever say belonged to me. I was more than grateful. Sometimes it felt like we were meant to be. More times, it felt like we placed ourselves together, minus the whole fate thing. She was the day to my night and being proud was an understatement when it came down to how much I saluted my queen for standing firmly in college for the sake of our lives. That was gonna be a foundation I praised at the end of the journey I had yet to be taken on.

Chapter 4
Silent Avenue
8:27 P.M

Finally, after a long day of driving around in Bleeko's shit, we touched the block. It wasn't usually an outstanding feeling to love and cherish the street your folks were murdered on, but it was still the same hood that made me the man that I was. I started dealing crack around the age of seventeen after I linked back in with Bleeko, but before then, I was a maniac with that pistol. Except I wasn't robbing. I was stankin' shit and leaving the forensics team to try and find out why. The only thing my mind used to be fixated on was redeeming my family's name. It was the hurt part of me that desired revenge. As I got older, I realized that a face with no case made it pretty evident where I would end up if I kept trying to guess on a miracle or answer to find my lucky victim.

As we pulled down in the corner store's parking lot, this nasty bitch named Nina was at Bleeko's window, knocking and talking like she didn't see that hard-ass glass wasn't about to move. This nigga was so stupid. He held his ear like he was really trying to hear her over that loud ass amplifier in his whip. I didn't even wanna be around her disrespectful ass, so I just excused myself from the car.

"Damn, Trap Baby. You act like ya daddy when you get in yo feelings. Ya lil bitch must ain't sucking ya dick, right?" Nina started popping her damn gums immediately.

Huffing lightly, I just stood and looked at the bitch. Her nasty black weave was dehydrated like a starving dog, and I know for a fact that she had this same fake ass Tina Turner-looking ass dress on for about three days straight. Nina was a chick that had great respect on the block for the money she kept throughout the nineties. She was more than just annoying.

41

Her ass was a nat. Always swerving around in business that wasn't hers and trying to eat off every damn plate she could. Her pale skin would make you think that she was white, but that was the drugs allowing her mixed side to stand out. She was half-Black and Spanish. The bitch had to be around forty-eight with a porn star body that would make Ice-T snatch her up for a lead run in his stable. Literally, after all the horses that had pumped inside of that, she still didn't have a scratch on her body. The hoe was on my bumper once like a NASCAR racer after she found out that Franklin was my dad. I could tell that he had an impact on her because she started to stick to me like gum under the bottom of a mattress until Kay-Kay nearly broke her neck one night in front of the block. She dragged her ass halfway up the street with an old fashion beat down.

"Nah. My girl don't suck it. She caresses and chokes on it just the way I like. You must be mad, bitch?" I replied while serving one of my usual customers.

"She doing all that and still ain't swallowed the whole thing. Mhm! I guess Mami's little mouth ain't big enough for all that Papi Chula." She laughed before jumping in the car with Bleeko.

Shaking my head, I started to stroll down the street just a little to see who was all out lurking. I could see Trevor and Dunk standing in front of the closed-down food factory for the homeless. That was their little spot to catch the quick sales that came from the cut, and they were also Bleeko's young shooters. Them fools had more bodies than a morgue. Reckless wasn't the word for the havoc they could easily cause if given the word. They earned their name on Silent Avenue and damn sure was trying to hold them crowns sturdy.

After strolling around for about twenty minutes, I made at least seven more sales and glanced at the clock. It was eight fifty-three, and I had to make sure I didn't get beat home.

Thumbing through the cash in my hands, I nearly like to pull my gun out to let loose when I felt a small tap on my shoulder. Turning around with the quickness, I spotted Cat standing behind me, looking around as if he was waiting on the Marta bus to pull up.

"What's good, Nephew?"

Exhaling, I put my bread up and laughed. "Man, Cat, you can't be doing that shit, man. You just like to make me pull the fire out on ya, old man."

"I don't care about no damn fire. I just wanted to see how my nephew was doing." He rubbed the top of his kitten's head gently.

Cat was like an uncle to me. He was the only homeless nigga on the block that had a gang of cats following him from sunup to sundown. At least five of those little fuckers. He used to always tell me stories of how him and my dad grew up in the same household. He definitely knew a lot of personal shit that only fam could know, so I never hesitated on embracing him and tossing some paper in his pocket if he ever asked. He always wore the same seven outfits throughout the week without changing his Coogi sweater. That nigga kept that bitch on during the winter and summer. The one thing I respected this old nigga about was that he took care of those damn cats like they were his biological children. All the change and money he gathered up throughout the day would get spent on a quart of milk or a large pack of tuna. It showed me that if a homeless man could still have responsibilities to take care of something, then I could maintain without having to do a lot of the things I was used to.

"Wassup with you, Cat? Tell me something good?" I held up a twenty-dollar bill.

"The sky is blue, and the police is white, still killing innocent black people, nephew. That's why I protect the animals.

They've adapted all the sense of the human and gave them the wild traits. No wonder the folks scared of us," he whispered like he was telling some top-secret information.

"Oh yeah, one more thing. Bleeko is some bullshit, nephew. Franklin wouldn't let you hang with that Barney ass nigga if he was still alive. Look at that nigga's skin. He's red like the devil." Cat's eyes were wide with hate as he took the money out of my hand.

"What's wrong with Bleeko, Unc? He ain't never done me wrong?" I asked out of curiosity. Every time I ran into Cat, he would always spill some dirty shit about Bleeko. I could tell from his infuriated expressions that whatever it was, it had to be personal. Anytime I asked Bleeko, he would just tell me that Cat was a bum ass family member who used to rob with them back in the days until he got on the smack. But as usual, neither wanted to speak on too much.

"You'll end up seeing it for yaself, nephew. Snakes have a nasty way of coming up out of that grass when you put the lawnmower blades down on that shit. Silent Avenue can't hide a loud ass nigga. Remember that," Cat said as he picked up two of the kittens, placing them inside of his sweater.

I just nodded to make sure he didn't snap on me and watched as he disappeared back behind the building. Cat was a weird, old-ass nigga, but he damn sho' had great sense. Not too many baseheads could tell you the movement that was going on in the hood without dropping too many details. Cat could give you the scoop without saying shit, and that alone was a blessing for me because niggas weren't accustomed to just making up shit when it came down to somebody that wasn't good for ya. That's just a lil thought I kept to myself regardless of what I heard.

Checking my watch again for the time, I knew that Kay-Kay was definitely on her way home from the job. I wanted to at least have a head start on getting the house together before she arrived. Bathwater, movie, bedspreads pulled back. Shit like that made her little coochie giggle for me.

Walking back up towards the top, I noticed Bleeko's car was still parked. It took me a second to figure out that Nina's nasty ass was still in the car trying to deactivate her game for a few bucks. Just as I was about to say fuck it and walk, her filthy ass came up out the front seat with a shitty smile like she just brushed her shit with Colgate and not Bleeko's drain babies.

"Don't hate, Trap Baby. I tried to offer you some." She left the passenger door open, strutting off slowly like a video vixen.

"You should have offered these car seats some plastic before sitting yo nasty ass down," I spat before jumping inside the car, shutting the door.

Bleeko was laughing and shit, but I truly didn't like that bitch. I could smell a grimy hoe all the way from another state, and she was the number one tourist.

"Wassup with you and Nina, man?

I looked at that nigga crazy like he was the one smoking that crack that was in his pockets. "Man, you know the word is that bitch had my dad setup back in the day. The only reason I ain't killed that hoe is because I ain't got no solid proof. I don't know what it is, but I can feel the dirtiness sliding from her tongue every time she comes around."

Bleeko grew quiet for a second, and I could tell he wanted to say something but quickly changed his mind. "Look, Melly. A lot of niggas will whisper on the block about shit they feel, not facts. Silent Avenue was really Silent Avenue back then. Motherfuckas saw shit but didn't speak on it. Period. No matter who asked. Nina didn't have shit to do with Franklin being murdered. That's just gossip, lil bro. I know this for a fact."

"What other facts you know then?" I kept my eyes on him with all seriousness. You could always feel when a nigga was preparing to lie about some shit just from their posture and the direction of the conversation. Instead of me pressing for answers, I faced the window, allowing that negative energy to pass through me. It seemed like Franklin always happened to be a sensitive subject around certain individuals. That shit made me feel more uneasy, but I still realized that my father left a nasty impact on certain individuals. Instead of placing gasoline over the fire, I remained quiet until Bleeko pulled his car into my driveway.

"Let me ask you something, Bleek?" I spoke just before I grabbed the door handle to step out.

"What's good, lil bro?"

"If somebody was ever trying to slime me out, would you tell me?" I turned back to look into his eyes.

"You sound crazy as fuck. I wouldn't have to tell you, 'cause whoever plays like that will get smoked where they stand, Melly. That's crazy." He frowned at me as if I assassinated his character.

"That's love, big bro." I embraced him with a brotherly handshake and smile. Stepping out of the car, I headed for the house and quickly allowed the happy expression to fade. The answer that I was just given proved to me one thing for sure. Still, I was gonna keep my balance and move like a true friend was supposed to do. In the end, it was all a dog-eat-dog world.

* * *

Kay-Kay

Pulling the car into our parking lot, I spotted the time that read 12:03 A.M. on my car radio. I was three hours late getting home, and Melly's French fries and burgers were beyond cold. After work, I ran to do a little last-second shopping with my mom for our camping trip. That twenty-minute mark stretched out to be three hours, and now I know this crazy-ass man was in the house probably having a talk with God and everybody in the world about how he was gonna kill me or throw me in the bottom of a lake if I didn't come home.

Grabbing all my bags, I got out of the car and headed inside. The lights were off in the house. By the time I sat down my things, I had found Melly's ass in the living room stretched out on the sofa. I walked over to him and could clearly see that he was uncomfortable in his sleep. He couldn't stop moving. Looking down at the glass table behind me, I picked up the small piece of paper with my name on it. There was a frowny face with the words, "I'm mad," resembling a child's handwriting.

I should jump on his ass, I thought before my eyes roamed down to his slight hard-on. His basketball shorts always made me turn into a dirty little freak for some reason. The night was still not over, and tomorrow was our camping trip where we would probably get no space, so I wasn't even about to waste any more time.

Pulling my hair up in a bun, I squatted down in front of Melly and whipped his dick clean out of them shorts. Before he could fully wake, I was easing him down my throat, slightly gagging just the way he liked it. Using two hands to rub the spit up his shaft, I bobbed my head smoothly on his member. I watched as his eyes fluttered open. He was huffing like he was so mad, but that tongue was calming his ass all the way back down to sleep mode. All he could do was gently rub the back of my head and grunt lightly every time I deep throated him. Melly's dick was a tear dropper. The one that could make your eyes water up like a bitch just got the news that her man wasn't coming home. I savored every time I got a chance to slide my mouth on his chocolate stick, and each time it tasted better. He spread his legs wider, allowing that dick to touch the back of my tonsils just how I liked. I could tell he was enjoying it from the way he rubbed my arched booty through the thin work scrubs.

I was shocked when he snatched the candy stick out of my mouth like I was just done sucking his shit. Moving behind me, he slowly pulled down my pants and slid my Snoopy boy shorts right to side. My pussy was throbbing like a heartbeat when he slid that monster inside my fatty.

"Ssss… Mhmmm!" I mashed my head into the couch when he spread my ass to go deeper. I could feel him digging in my shit like he was looking for diamonds, and she didn't hesitate to talk back to him with every stroke he delivered.

"Where the fuck you been?" he mumbled aggressively, slamming a hard hand down on my apple bottom, causing me to bust immediately. I could feel his dick slide out to the tip and reenter me viciously before he latched on to my tiny waist.

"I was shoppinggg, daddyyy." I looked back into his eyes, knowing that shit was gonna spark a blaze in his adrenaline.

"No call, No message. Huh?" He teased me with a slow deep thrust while rubbing on my titty.

"No... I wanted...to make you mad," I panted through the pain he was already delivering.

"Okay." He was now pushing my back in deeper, so the kitty faced him like a head-up fight. "Say you sorry!" He leaned back, digging inside me deeper.

My eyes rotated in my head like the lottery balls inside of that giant plastic container they used to reveal the numbers. My shit was gushing cum out by the second from the way he was mistreating the pussy, and the pit of my stomach said that I had to piss, but I knew it was probably this nigga touching my bladder. The room was quiet besides my light moans and the heavy sound of my pussy creaming in delight. My ass was bouncing roughly against his pelvis as he bullied his way inside of my guts.

"I'll fucking kill you, Kay-Kay." He licked the side of my neck while a few of his fingers manipulated my love button.

I wanted to scream out, do it, but I didn't have the voice to back it up. I could see from the mirror that sat to my right how far he was putting it in me, and I was praying that my heart didn't give out before he fucked the lights out of the body I was currently still living in.

"Stretch yo hands out in front of you and keep that ass in the air." I could feel his strokes getting freakier.

Doing what I was told, I reached out in front of me. His fingers rubbed around my kitty lips, and he was definitely playing in that second overflow of vanilla passion I released. I closed my eyes, receiving the rest of my ass spanking. Forty-five minutes later, I found myself riding Melly's dick cowgirl style in our bedroom. His shit was starting to hurt, and every time I came down on it, h was meeting me with an up stroke. My ass bounced freely on him, and I could tell that he was about to bust one from the way his face was balling up. Arching my apple, I rode that dick with a purpose for those last few seconds until I drained every drip of sperm his crazy ass had to offer.

Melly didn't waste any time pulling me down on the bed with him. I could feel the wet spots on our sheets, and he was just always comfortable with laying in it.

"Where you going?" he asked me when I raised his arm to get out of the bed.

"To the shower, crazy man. Yo sticky ass need to be following me." I kissed his lips and started to navigate through the darkness in our dresser.

"Nah, I like these sticky ass sheets. Leave me be." He farted and rolled over.

"Eww, Melly! What the fuck? Get yo stink ass out of bed and come shower. You smell like you need a laxative boy." I grabbed my nose and quickly headed for the bathroom.

Thinking about our family trip tomorrow, I could only imagine the acrimony my father was ready to indulge in with Melly. He wasn't the best when it came to accepting the fact that I was rising up to become my own woman, with my own family just as he and my mother did. He felt that I was still his baby Kayona. The little princess who wanted an Easy-Bake Ovens and Barbies for Christmas. Unfortunately, those times had passed. I could never stop being the baby in his eyes, but Melly was now my baby, and that was a strong factor that I wanted him to grow to love with because it wasn't about to change regardless of if the trip was a success or not. I just prayed that it didn't take Melly from his comfort zone on us leaving Atlanta for good. That was my only focus. Saving him from the streets that had already taken so much away.

Chapter 5
Melly

As I stepped out on the front porch, the sun was shaded behind a pillow of clouds forcing the darkness to rise as the new day and the streets were nearly empty. The sight of a car riding smoothly down my block with the music bumping, forced me to listen to the Tupac song that was spilling through the speakers.

"Come with me! Hail Mary! What do we have here now? Do you wanna ride or die? La'da da-da-da-da-da... I ain't a killer but don't push me. Revenge is like the sweetest joy next to getting pussy!"

As the car grew closer, I noticed that it was a 2003 candy-apple red Caddy. I could see a nigga in the driver's seat, nodding his head like he was the king of the world. The face of a young boy could be seen in the passenger seat just as they reached the edge of my home. My vision rotated to the pistol that was now rising in my hand, and the face of a bloody old woman flashed quickly through my head before I started releasing shots from the gun.

Boc! Boc! Boc! Boc! Boc! Boc! Boc!

The bullets ripped through the Cadillac's window, hastily striking the child and man inside. I watched them both bleed profusely and slump to the side as Tupac's voice boomed louder. "Wake up, Melly! The nightmare is over. Wake up!"

Jumping up from the lucid dream that was just pumping through my head, I viewed Kay-Kay standing over me with tears nearly ready to fall from her eyes. Her hands were up in a defensive motion, and that's when I noticed the gun that was in my hand aiming directly for her.

"Melly, please wake up!" she pleaded with fear shifting throughout her body.

I could see my finger on the trigger, caressing it as if I were ready to take the love of my life away from me forever. Without hesitation, I tossed it towards the wall and jumped up to console her. My hands grabbed ahold of Kay-Kay's cheek-bones forcing her to look at me. "Baby, I'm so, so sorry. You know that I would never hurt you. You know that, right?" I gazed down into her teary face with grief that weighed on me unmercifully.

"Melly, look." She pointed her shaky hand towards the closet, where I had obviously released a few slugs in my sleep. That shit had a thick pain of regret circling inside my chest, and all I could imagine was me accidentally shooting Kay-Kay. The thought was so dreadful it had me ready to cry, feeling like she was struck instead of being missed.

Kissing her forehead numerous times, I hugged around her waist and realized that she was dressed for our camping trip with my parents-in-law. A pair of small dickie shorts was hiked up on her butt. A fitted T-shirt that read, "Green Leaves and Sticks Are My Friends," was tucked in neatly, and her natural hair was curled down to the back with perfection. Her brown eyes were studying me, and I was surely gonna need a median to balance my spazz out this morning if I didn't plan on losing the same woman that I fought so hard to have beside me.

"Melly, we have to get you some help, baby. I'm scared that you might hurt yourself, or me if we don't try and work on seeing what can lead you to break out of these disturbing dreams."

She was asking me more than telling, and even though I didn't want to debate about it at the time, Kay-Kay was right. So, I just nodded and kissed her hands passionately. "I will baby. I'll accept the help."

"Good." She stood up on her toes to kiss my lips. Watching her walk over to the corner, picking up my gun with a straight face. Her eyes met mines. "I'll be holding this from now on until you really need it. Go ahead and get dressed. My parents will be here in thirty minutes." She dropped it in her purse and headed out of the room, leaving me to myself.

I moved to the bathroom and turned on the hot water from the sink. Dashing it across my face a few times, I tried my best to envision the faces that were riding in the car of my dream. *Why did I kill them?* It all felt so real that I didn't know what to think. The one thing that I wouldn't forget was the bloody face of that old woman. It was my second time spotting her image in my dreams, and I knew for a fact that I wasn't being chased by no damn ghosts; neither was Kay-Kay's shit haunted. It was a mystery that wouldn't leave me alone, no matter how bad I tried to keep good thoughts running through my head at night. Part of me felt that it was my family's demise that wouldn't stop eating at me, but Kay-Kay felt that I needed a closer relationship with God. Religion was my only downfall. I truly didn't know who to pray to.

* * *

Detective Solomon

It was no earlier than 8:30 A.M. according to my Tudor wristwatch when I finally seen this asshole, Bleeko, pull back up in front of the Sanabella's Restaurant on Silent Avenue. I had been patrolling the neighborhood from the Zone One Precinct of the Atlanta Police Department for three years now, and I still had yet to meet an arrogant *Sanford and Son*-looking muthafucka like him. He moved around, enforcing his little power throughout the youth. Tricking them with money and drug bags like he was just a real entrepreneur around the fucking city. Dirty-ass hood nigga type shit. The department had received numerous calls about the clown, and no matter how many times I tried to be the savior of the dumb dickheads of the century, they proved to me why I'm so stupid for even coming up with the concept of interfering with street justice. At least that's what the goodie, candy in the ass cops believed. I've always felt different. Growing up on this side of town would make any fool jump into the belly of the streets. The area was infested with drugs and congested with contaminating liars and disease passers. My life was brought up on the north side around the Doraville and Dunwoody areas. I still achieved all the goals possible in school just to reach the career to chase the same bad guys that I once craved to be like.

Watching the idiot and his two puppies, Trevor and Dunk, walk inside of the small orange One Shop Corner Store, I pulled my cruiser over the railroad tracks and mashed the gas gently until I reached the parking lot where these fools were designated. I already knew that I was dealing with some dangerous individuals, so playing the nice guy role would have to wait until I was really able to grasp their attention.

Right as I entered the door, I spotted Bleeko and Dunk purchasing a few items at the counter. Their eyes were focused on the young and pretty cashier that was working behind the counter, and I could clearly see the handles of the pistols they carried dangling freely on their waist. Trevor's eyes were the first to lock in on mines as he protruded out of the freezer aisle. He could see the fire in my eyes and knew if he even thought about trying me, I wouldn't hesitate to burn his ass like a cup of Listerine. Of course, he had to be a retard and risk everything for these two stupid dogs by yelling out my presence.

"Bleekoo, Twelve!"

By the time he was able to jolt back down the store aisle, I was on Mr. Bleeko's ass like a pair of tighty-whities.

Grabbing his ass by the wrist, I slammed him down to the ground and slapped him in a pair of cuffs.

"God damnn! What the fuck is this, Solomon?" he asked me when his fake ass Versace frames crumbled from the impact.

Removing my gun, I pointed it forcefully at the stomach of the man they called Dunk. "Get the fuck down right now before I put ya bitch ass on a colostomy bag!"

He was biting on his bottom lip like he had to think about it.

"Now!" I squinted my eyes with a little more bass in my voice.

Watching a nasty smirk slide across his face, he placed his hands on the top of his head and got on the ground. As I quickly moved over to place him in cuffs, the sneaky little bitch Trevor broke for the door. I raised my gun to pop his ass but realized that I didn't have a liable cause, so I allowed his fate to be decided the next time I ran across him. Slapping the clinks on Dunk's wrists, I removed his gun and placed it in my second hip holster.

Moving over to Bleeko, I did the same thing. Looking at the pretty handgun I removed from his possession, I shook my head with a whistle. "Mr. June aka Memphis Bleeko. This is a nice ass gun, my nigga. How much you buy it for?" I asked, rubbing a hand across my bald head.

"Man, come on, Solomon. What the fuck is this about? I stay out of ya way, and I ain't moved past them punk ass railroad tracks in yo lil territory. We had an agreement!" he snarled with anger written on his face.

"First of all, you need to lower some of that bass in your voice down, boy. I could've smoked y'all stupid ass niggas and told the coroner to take ya ass around to the nearest morgue," I mentioned before bending down next to him and his flunky. I could see that he wanted to make a smart remark, but he knew that I could easily blast his ass out. After all, they made the so-called rules out on Silent Avenue. Instead of kicking the belligerent shit, his posture calmed.

"Come on, Solomon. I been clean, man. You ain't had a run-in with me in six months. Cut me some fucking slack, bruh! That's what you want, the guns?" he asked as if I was gonna reinstate them the right to be a felon and carry a firearm.

Huffing with pity, I chuckled. "The guns became mine when you allowed them to be visible, idiot. If I was any other cop, maybe even a bright-skin, I would've got away with pumping your damn brains on the pavement. I've been getting calls on the radio every four hours about you. The bullshit that you're causing on this hot ass block. The same block that I've asked you numerous times to take a break from," I explained as I checked his pockets and sat him up straight.

"Let's be real, Solomon. Half of these same motherfuckers that's calling you about me are probably the same bitches buying my dope. I'm a hood figure. What the fuck do you expect? We aren't kids, and you've known me for years. What's changed besides the amount of my savings?" He gave me a look that said bribery was on his mind.

Knowing the games Bleeko played, he was trying to talk his way out of a first-class trip to the county on weapon charges. I never respected a lot of his actions as a man, but I've always witnessed the help he's offered to the low- lives of the community. It was one of the only reasons I always allowed him to receive a break on my end. I wasn't the average Atlanta police officer. Hell, half of my family was incarcerated and involved with the dark world. That still didn't defeat the fact that I had a job to enforce and secure.

"Sometimes, I feel like you don't even respect the name of your own hood dumb-dumb. My hands are tied with the bullshit, Bleeko. I can't keep saving you and your little fuck buddies. I have a boss. A boss who wants your ass buried in prison for a few decades. You're on a short leash mother-fucker!" I pointed at his face before removing the cuffs from his wrists.

He stood up from the floor, dusting off his clothes with a satisfied smile. "When have I ever bucked on you, Solomon?"

"When have you ever took heed, boy? Stop using your fake ass intelligence and open up them big ass elephant ears. I have no room left for compassion, and I refuse to keep in-dulging with this stupidity you're pulling. The next time I get a call over my scanner or a paper on my desk about you, Jack-son, I'm coming, and I'm taking all your little ball-holding ass workers down with you."

I looked over at the young fella, Dunk, and quickly ad-dressed him before removing the cuffs. "That goes for you too, son. Stop holding this man's nuts and find something success-ful to do!"

All they could do was nod0 and salute me like I gave a damn about that. I wasn't a big dawg in the hood. I damn sure wasn't a dictator, but I refused to keep allowing my coworkers to slap those bracelets on these boys' wrists all because of them being forced to live in an area that was labeled hell on earth. Of course, there was a choice, but there was also an overseer who gave the authority to see if that choice was al-lowed in a power-struck country. An overseer who I knew would keep their chokehold on the African race until the color drained from our flesh. That was a day I refused to be a part of, regardless of how much I stood on my beliefs of living like a law-abiding citizen.

Taking Dunk out of the cuffs, I nodded towards the beau-tiful young lady behind the counter and placed my eyes back on Bleeko. "Be sure to tell your little friend, Trevor, when I catch him, his ass is going for a ride down to Rice Street. I don't like runners," I warned him, sliding out of the front door quicker than I came.

As the sun caressed against my face, I placed my shades on and slid in the front seat of my cruiser. I could see the two of them staring at me through the filthy plastic window. Bleeko's grin said that he was surely gonna be a problem, but in the end, I was damn sure prepared for his ass to slip.

Chapter 6
Melly

We had been walking up this side trail for almost thirty minutes, and now I was starting to pour sweat like a donkey that took eighty days to make it through the Sahara Desert. My hands were filled with all Kay-Kay's crazy knickknacks, and not to mention the shit her dad, Benjamin, had me carrying like I was the caddy man for his golfing clubs. It seemed like her mama was the only one to show a nigga that I was loved. She saw me edging towards death during our walk and thought to come to offer me something to drink. Right after the first two swallows of her famous lemonade, she reminded me that I was getting no slack.

"Come on, Meltavious. Pick that stuff back up, baby. We are already here. Ain't no need for slowing down now," Mrs. Wilcox said that like she was the one toting ten bags of miscellaneous shit for a one-night camping trip. In the end, it was for Kay-Kay, so I refused to show any emotions as if I were dissatisfied to be in that spot with them at that exact moment.

Once we finally made it to flat ground, I allowed the things to fall from my grasp and nearly flopped down on top of it.

"Aww. It's okay, baby. Go ahead and get you some rest." Kay-Kay laughed before bending down to kiss my lips. That one peck caused me to look in between her legs at the hotdog bun that was poking from her shorts. I had to make sure her mom and pops weren't looking before I rubbed a sweaty hand across her kitty. "You owe me."

"Melly!" She balled up her lips with a shocking smile. "Not here. Don't start!"

I looked at her like she was going halfway crazy. "Who? Girl, I just sat here and carried all that shit up this rock. We're definitely smacking skins tonight, yo."

"What if they hear us?"

I shrugged. "They probably gonna be in their own tent groaning and crying right after they think we're sleeping; watch."

Kay-Kay wiggled a finger towards me before walking off to assist her mother with preparing the food for us all. I grabbed that dick with wide eyes so she could know I was painting that ass tonight, whether if it was gonna be in that tent or us walking back down this rock to get in the backseat of our car.

Just as I was thinking about finding me a nice spot to sit my ass down and hop on my phone, Mr. Benjamin brought his ass over by me with a stale face. "Resting is for when the night falls, son. You need to be grabbing that tent so we can fix these things on up. You ain't gon' be no poor excuse of a son around me." He waved his hand around like he was just running shit. He was an old fake ass Isley Brothers looking nigga. From the light grey baby hair that was barely hanging on. The old black pimp stick with a lion's head on the handle. He always kept a pair of suspenders on with every suit or slacks, and the man had a different color Kango to match with everything he fucking wore. His whole damn style was aggravating me, but once again, it was all for the sake of my Queen. After almost eight years of a successful relationship, Kay-Kay and I finally decided to start thinking of marriage, and that's when Mr. Benjamin started to pull his boxers up in his ass. Instead of being a good supporter, his statements and actions began to portray that he wanted Kay-Kay to probably change her mind. We never too much bonded until I started to gain a better relationship with Mrs. Wilcox. Hell, the old man even thought I was beating his wife's back out at one point. She became close to me and knew for a fact that I was willing to die about her daughter, but in Mr. Benjamin's eyes, I was trying to remove his girl's cleanliness from his world. In a way, it made me respect him because I knew he was being sure to secure the safety of the two women in his life. Still in all, I wanted him to realize that another man was now in the picture, and I cared just as much as he did.

"I got ya, Mr. Benjamin." I exhaled before standing to my feet.

"After you're done, I need to sit and have a word with you. Alone," he clarified with a serious face. I knew that it had to be something important because we barely had a small conversation throughout the years. I could see Kay-Kay watching me with an inquisitive eye. Her lips were mumbling a few words that I couldn't hear, but it clearly looked as if she were telling me not to fuck up. True enough, I could be a hard ass sometimes, but I was usually good when it came down to shit like family bonding or making someone smile. I was the life of any household. Everybody included me with nearly everything that had any dealings with enjoying themselves when I came around. I still couldn't figure out the fact why Kay-Kay's old man gave me such an excruciating time whenever I tried to embrace him.

After helping set up the tents, which took me a little bit over an hour, Benjamin and I headed out in the woods to find a nice bundle of burning logs that could last throughout the night. It hadn't even passed five in the afternoon, and I had already found myself with seven cuts on my hand, a banging ass migraine, and some soaked ass socks for jumping in this large ass puddle of water that I thought was just a dirty pile of leaves and mud. I tried my best not to show my anger, especially when this fat ass nigga was passing gas through the entire damn trail. I had to turn my head while trying to keep up without having to eat the shitty air. By the time we were back at the station where our tents were located. Kay-Kay and Mrs.

Wilcox already had our small section set up nicely. I could see the bowl of watermelon that was searching for my dry ass tongue, and the smell of some delicious ass burgers made a nigga's stomach talk like a baby was having a comedy show inside of my shit.

"Bae, taste this!" I turned around to Kay-Kay, placing a spoon of potato salad up to my lips.

Of course, I bit it off the spoon like it was the most delicate piece of food that I would ever taste. When the real thump from the salad started to kick in, I looked at her curiously. "Who made this?"

She just started smiling like I knew the answer. "Boy, you know I got my own special recipes too."

"Girl, I don't know nothing. Yo food had some special nasty…"

She slapped me across the shoulder before I could finish. I had to laugh because she knew that her and cooking fought more than any husband and wife. "I'm just talking, Kaycake. The potato salad is great. Your daddy killed my spirit for any meal on the way back."

"What do you mean?" she asked while following me back to the area her parents sat.

"Because he damn near dropped a turd on every poison oak bush. That man needs to go and check his draws for real."

Kay-Kay tried to cover up her enormous smile from my dumb-ass comment, and of course, her mother wanted in on the convo once we finally reached her and Benjamin.

"What's funny, Kayona? I need a good laugh too."

"Yeah, Kay-Kay. Tell mama what's funny, baby. I'm sure she and Benjamin would love to know what we have on our minds." I laid back on the blanket with a fat ass smirk as all the attention went directly to her.

She huffed and squinted her eyes at me with dislike. "Well, Melly and I were talking about a dirty trail of turds always falling around us."

I sat up quick as hell, thinking she was about to say something crazy.

"Trail of turds? Kayona, what are you talking about?" Benjamin butted in.

Of course, she started to laugh at my scary ass before continuing on with her lie.

"I'm talking about the dirty mess that keeps falling around the environment we currently live in. We're growing faster now, and I don't want to wait too late before I find a true place to settle and call home." She was picking with the edges of her hair like she did when we were in high school.

"So let me guess, you're talking about leaving Atlanta again?" He lowered his head disappointingly.

Kay-Kay rubbed his hands with a bright smile. "Yes, daddy. I am, but that doesn't mean that I'm leaving you and mommy forever. Melly and I will always be down here to visit on holidays, and I'll also make a trip down here every other month to make sure y'all are behaving."

"That doesn't warm my spirit, Kayona. What if you're not protected? How will you survive without being close to us?" Benjamin asked like I just wasn't talking about shit. He knew that I was beyond dedicated when it came to taking care of his daughter, so the comment was meant to be a low blow.

I could see Mrs. Wilcox lean up from his lap, looking back with a disapproving smirk. "Benjamin, you know, just like I do that these kids love each other. They're gonna have to eventually find their own route sooner or later. I support both of you, and I'm gonna be waiting back here for some grandbabies of my own to spoil." She was blushing at me as her husband bit down on his sand which.

"Exactly, mama. I'm on my last course for school, and after this degree, I wanna be able to start over and build my own office in Colorado. I know that it's quite a distance from Georgia, but it's a start."

"And I suppose that you can survive on the back end with Meltavious saving his drug money?" Benjamin's weak-ass remark forced me to get up and walk off. I couldn't take it anymore. I refused to sit back and let him belittle me all because he came up differently than I could.

"Melly, no. He didn't mean it like that bay." Kay-Kay tried to grab my arm, but I objected. I didn't need her following behind me, and I wasn't about to throw it up in her face that this shit would go totally wrong when it came down to her father and me coming together on anything.

Kicking the small rocks in front of my shell toe Adidas as I walked, I found a small stump about fifty feet away from our camping spot and took a seat. The view gave me just enough sight to gaze out at the beaming sun and large park. Judging someone never mattered to a motherfucker that had a silver spoon coming up. I know that was part of the reason I never truly got along with Kay-Kay's dad. He was a college dude, and my father was a robber. The times when he was coming home with schoolwork, my pops was breaking down packs and guns. It showed me in a certain way why our vision refused to click. His mind was set on having her a preppy and bougie life, but that wasn't how she planned on living. A part of me wondered what the hell I had to do to show that my position was grounded. It was like trying to prove to a baby that goo-goo-gah-gah wasn't a word. Truly, I was drained from it all and didn't give a damn how he felt. The respect was only there for the sake of his daughter. Nothing more. The small aggravating situation boiled me to the point where I took a seat on the grass and dazed into the passing misty clouds. Not too long after, I was slightly dozing off into a light sleep. Waking up forty-five minutes later, I could see that the sun was slowly decreasing towards the horizon. Obviously, everyone decided to keep their distance because no one had yet to come down and rescue me from the ugly slump I was currently feeling weighing down on me. Deciding to tighten up and head back towards my woman, I got up, dusting myself off before making my way up the slanted hill. When I reached the top, I could see Kay-Kay and her mother occupying our tent with their own bonding moment. I had to walk past Benjamin in order to get there, but I wasn't gonna even pay the nigga no mind as I paced through like he wasn't sitting around a warm ass campfire alone.

"Melly, let me have a word with you, son," he spoke, but never took his eyes off the burning blaze that danced in front of his pupils.

Huffing, I thought about telling him to jump in a casket and let me kick that bitch off the side of this big ass mountain, but instead, I folded once again. Lowering my head. I took a deep breath and grabbed a seat directly next to him on the wooden bench. I could see that he wanted to apologize, but that old nigga was so stuck in his ways that he had to make a joke from all of the nonsense.

"I know you're thinking about stuffing me over into this burning fire, but I'm warning you. My skin's too thick, so I might not cook well." He forced me to laugh at the comment.

His words were shortened for a few more seconds before he finally looked over at me and proved that he could be a real man when it came down admitting his faults. "I'm sorry, Meltavious. I know that I could probably be hard sometimes. Well, more than some. But what's the probability of the fathers out in this world who don't give a rat's ass about their children, son? Kayona is my princess. It seemed just like yesterday where I was walking with her through Walter White Elementary School. Now I'm watching her stroll across the stage, accepting her college degree in dentistry. It makes me wonder how much time I have to build with my baby before there is nothing left to build," he questioned with a face that said he already knew the answer.

"Mr. Benjamin, I know that it may seem like I'm inconsistent with the things that you expect to see out of a young man, or maybe I have a few traits that I know will eventually have to fall in order to have a fruitful relationship with Kay-Kay. I know that everything takes time, but I know one thing for sure. I love Kayona Wilcox with every ounce of blood that's flowing through my veins at this moment. I'll protect. I will kill, and I will die, if necessary, about caring and providing for her at any cost. And nobody will be able to stop that, Mr. Benjamin. Not even you."

I was looking straight at his face to see if I could sense any anger or malice flowing through his words so that I could quickly end the conversation where it started. To my surprise, he respected it.

"I never said that I didn't know that, son. I could tell by the way you follow her around; you're head over hills." He chuckled before reaching his hands out to the fire feeling the warm heat gust from the flames. "I just want to make sure that you have prosperity and sincerity when you commit your life to her. Being a man comes with more than just protecting your spouse. It also follows with making the right decisions. Knowing when an argument is lost and respecting her bossy, but somewhat bold decisions on what she feels is best. I'm not saying allow her to take your dignity as a man, but allow her to understand that a black woman's word also holds weight too. I just want to see her rise and glow as any other Queen who's with the best athlete or lawyer. If my baby's desire is with you, then I can be man enough to respect it. My ass is too old to use my hands to check it anymore, but if I get close enough, I got a good haymaker that'll take Tyson down." He shot a fake jab at my arm.

Chuckling, I embraced him with a firm handshake, but my eyes showed the seriousness in my next statement. "I just want to be family, sir. I wouldn't want to see me and Kay-Kay leave off and travel through a tunnel of no return. I would like to see you and Mrs. Wilcox by our side as our parents, watching their children making a bigger step into this world. Nothing more."

Mr. Benjamin held on firmly and nodded with assurance. "Just keep that promise golden for my daughter, and I'll give you the shirt off my back if you asked, son."

"Thanks, Mr. Benjamin."

"No need to thank me." He waved my ass off with a smile. "Now go and get your little cry baby, so she can let my wife come back to me. I'm getting lonely out here." His eyes glanced back at them as if he was hoping that his two favorite girls weren't plotting on boycotting his love.

Making my way over to the tent, I peeped my head inside, and Mrs. Wilcox ceased the small talk immediately. "Well damn, Melly. I am your mother-in-law, you know. I got rights over you too, boy. Let me start to address things first before you decide to start walking away while I'm defending you, punk." She raised a balled fist at me.

Climbing down inside the spacious sleeper, I hugged her neck and placed a kiss on her cheek. "I know, mama. Mr. Benjamin and I just needed a little time to gather our thoughts individually. All should be well, and we're trying to weld this broken piece of aggravating tension without actually trying to find a solution for where to mold it down firmly. He's out there asking for you now." I grinned, tilting my head out to the old playa. He was wearing this cheesy ass smirk like he just knew Mama Wilcox was about to hit the gas back over to him. I watched as he showed that my position was grounded. Maybe I hadn't gotten enough game on being a playa yet, because Mrs. Wilcox jerked slightly. I could see the little freaky side lingering right off her face.

"I gotta go, babies. It's time for me and ya daddy to have our own little talk." She winked at us before hoping her little balloon-body self up quicker than a badass three-year-old in search of the fresh grocery bags coming through the house.

Kay-Kay shook her head with a smile before zipping us inside our cozy little tent. "I guess that's our cue that they'll be having some fun tonight."

I leaned back, laughing like a motherfucka. "You know how old people act when they get steamed up, bae. Hell, I'm glad, cause yo daddy act like he ain't had no ass in the last twelve years."

"You so silly, but I'm glad that you were able to at least get an understanding with him." Kay-Kay kissed me and cuddled her head into my chest.

I didn't want to rush and agree with her because there was no telling how long the mutual agreement would stick between me and his old ass. I didn't like the fact that I had disputes with my woman's father, but I also knew that it was no such thing as a suburban raised family embracing the local hood drug dealer upon introduction.

"I feel like things could get better only if he's really sincere about accepting our relationship. At the end of the day, I'm not marrying him. So, his emotions will have to remain in his heart instead of on his sleeve."

"I understand, Melly. Regardless of how my dad feels, I'll still be right beside you until we depart from this earth. You're my heart, my soul, and that alone means everything to me, whether my father hates your guts or accepts you as his own biological son."

She was gazing up in my eyes like that statement came from the pit of her soul. It was the reason I treated her better than any royal Queen across the globe. Not only was she determined to make our love shine like the morning rising into the sky, but she was willing to turn away from the ones who brought her into this world to prove it. I was about to explain how much I cherished her when a distant moan from Mrs. Wilcox escaped through the air. I thought that I might have been tripping, but Kay-Kay sat up with her sonic ears as if she heard E.T. break through the ozone layer to enter the earth. We both were frozen in place, waiting for another sign that we were accurate on our theory.

"Oh, Benjaminnn," her voice sounded off again.

Kay-Kay's eyes locked with mine, and we both smiled. I knew that the old heads wouldn't be able to hold out, and I could see the thought that was swirling around in my Baby's head. Without hesitation, we both started to fumble hastily to remove our clothes. I was leaning in for kisses and had a mouth full of titties before she could even take her bra off good enough.

"Melly, slow down. I don't want them to hear us," Kay-Kay snickered as I rushed to snatch off her itty-bitty shorts.

"You should have tried to tell ya parents the same thing," I smirked before turning on music from my cellphone and dropping my boxers.

Chapter 7
Two Days Later
Bleeko

Walking through Melly's bedroom door, I caught this nigga staring in the mirror with a smile like he was Victor Sweet from the film *Four Brothers*. The clean-ass Salvatore Ferragamo sweatsuit he wore was all black with white trimmings trailing down the side, and his feet sported a pair of clean hightop Balenciaga's. Moving over to his dresser, I grabbed the bottle of Yves Saint Laurent Cologne, dabbing a little on my wrist and neck. "God damn, Melly. You've been getting dressed for an hour, lil nigga. The fucking club will be an elderly home by the time we get in that muthafucka!"

He ignored me, rubbing all through his waves and shit. This man was a real bug when it came to being perfect. I didn't notice the silver bracelet that was on his wrist until he raised his left arm.

"What the fuck is that?" I balled up my face at the shitty piece of jewelry.

Melly's eyes rotated down to it with a smile. "You mean my bracelet? I got it for Christmas when I was a lil one. It's nice, right?"

"Yeah, Maybe for Kay-Kay or my sister, Fanta. That shit looks like it's for a girl, lil bruh. Take that shit off." I dug in my pocket pulling out my spare gold Submariner Rolex and placed it on his opposite wrist.

"Man, my mama gave me this. I thought it was clean, and it means something special to me, Bleeko."

"Well, let it be special in your own time, Melly Mel. You going out with big bro tonight. You gotta trust me. The type of spot we're walking in, they will think you're a male prostitute or a cop with that costume ass jewelry, man. We don't

71

need that type of lame-ass vibe mixing in on our aura, baby boy." I patted his shoulder and headed back towards the living room.

Exhaling, I had to shake my head and remember that Melly wasn't on point with a lot of things like I was. People preyed on certain shit like weak niggas or different appearances when you lived a life of fuckery and hatred. It was natural for the most, but with Melly, he was more of a specific target on the strength of his dad, Franklin.

"So, what club we heading to?" He stepped into the living room looking like a 1980s corner hustler. All he was missing was a few diamond rings and a fake ass gold tooth. The young nigga was fly, though.

"I wanna slide through to Lacure or The Mansion. I was supposed to meet up with a few cats from the nawf to lock in with Big Sal. If I bag this connect, we can be slanging birds across the city like pigeons that be downtown," I explained as we walked out of the house and jumped inside my 2018 Ram truck.

"Why the hell you ain't never let me meet this nigga, Big Sal, yet, man? I'm not trying to be working for you forever, Bleeko. God damn."

I turned to look at this nigga and shook my head.

"You must wanna have a baby by this nigga or some, man?"

Melly didn't like that shit. I could see his nostrils flare up, and he huffed like he ain't have no more kicking it, but that's exactly how I wanted him to feel.

"Man, you geeking, Bleeko. Stop talking to me like that, man."

He was staring into my eyes like he was daring me to say that shit again. You know I'm a realist, so I couldn't spell it out no other way. "Nah, lil bro. I explained this shit once already. Sal ain't meant for you to meet. What the fuck is you not hearing? Just 'cause you feel like getting off a couple of OZs is sufficient enough to be around this nigga who is dropping loads off on the entire city, you're wrong, Melly. This man doesn't trust motherfuckers at all. And if you keep begging for a damn chance just to say hey to the fucking man, you might get me, and you cut off. He's wishy-washy like a bitch, and right now, I know how to maneuver around this fool until we can bag a top position around this bitch. Look around, Melly." I waved my hand around at the street as we drove down towards the block. "We practically got every human being around Silent Avenue copping from us."

"True, but that doesn't mean I'm trying to have everybody on Silent Avenue in my business. I'm trying to rise and grind a little harder, my nigga. I got a life too, and I damn sure ain't about to be hustling on the block for the next five decades. I'm not hurting, but I'm not about to sit here and act like I'm straight enough to buy Kay-Kay no damn island and resort in Turks and Caicos, nigga. I'm ready to hang this shit up, Bleeko." He folded his arms like that was his New Year's resolution or some shit.

I understood his wishes, and it was nothing but respect for wanting to do better when your so-called had a bitch that was ready to hold ya down and do the whole family thing. I also knew that this hoe, Kay-Kay, had this nigga's nose wide open like a Walmart parking lot. She literally walked around with this Melly's balls in her purse, and he was so in love that it was blinding him to abandon the same streets that was feeding her. As I pulled down into the liquor store, I parked the car and forced a smile over to my young nigga. "I know shit might not seem like it's gonna bubble for you, baby boy. But you gotta know that I'm with you, not against you. If I eat, you eat. Ya hear me?"

He went to grinning from ear to ear, knowing that I wasn't bluffing about my promise. Even though I didn't try to show too much emotion when it came to the game, Melly was like a little brother to me. Plus, I could never forget the olive branch that his dad, Franklin, showed me when I was a curious hustler coming up in these streets. I was gonna be sure to show love and break bread whether he chose to leave the block today or stay out on this bitch until he was sixty.

Climbing out of the driver seat of my truck, I looked around at the moving traffic pacing up and down the hood. It was around nine-thirty, and I had tik make sure Melly and I were feeling extra good before we made our presence in this damn club. If I would have been on point, I'd probably seen the three suckas that were eyeballing me like the next *America's Top Model* before I made it inside. My mind was so focused on that paper the new plug could bring in, I nearly forgot that I had some smoke that still had yet to clear. After buying a bottle of Belvedere, I made my way back out the front door and quickly froze. I could see the three niggas creeping close to my truck, and that's when my eyes landed on Lonnie's big brother, raising his gun. Melly could see the look on my face, and before I could remove my gun off my hip, he sent a bullet through the back of my truck's window, forcing lil bro to duck for cover.

Boom!

The bottle of liquor fell from my hand, and my gun started to talk back without hesitation.

Poc! Poc! Poc! Poc! Poc!

I aimed recklessly, trying to splat whichever one of those bitches I could. I could hear them niggas' shit responding back, forcing me to edge towards the side of the store and fall. One of my bullets found a home in Lonnie's brother's shoulder, forcing him to drop his pistol. I jumped back to my feet, steadily pulling my trigger like it was the end. That's when I saw Melly slide out of the passenger seat and place a bullet straight into one of those bitches' skulls.

Boom!

I watched as his brain sprayed across the concrete before he crumbled to the ground. Before he could a good aim at Lonnie's brother, his little henchmen saved his life by running him back towards the black Nissan that was waiting for them by the edge of the street. Melly still didn't let up.

Boom! Boom!

He released two more shots, striking the back tire before these fuck niggas jumped inside their whip and smashed off with sparks flying from the rim.

The small distant screams could be heard loud and clear as people ducked for cover and cleared the block within a few seconds. As I stepped from the side of the building with my pistol still aimed, I could see Melly standing in the center of the parking lot with his gun lowered. He was staring out at a woman that cried in the middle of our four-way.

"Pleassee. Noo Godd. Someone get me some hellppp! Pleasee," she pleaded while holding a small little girl no older than the age of four in her arms. I could see the dark blood stain that was pouring from her back. A small gasp escaped my lips because I knew for a fact that I was the one who accidentally fired the bullet. It was the first thing my eyes caught when I fell on the side of the liquor store. My feet felt like glue, but I couldn't allow us to stand there and get them cuffs slapped on our wrist for something that was out of our control.

Running over to Mell, a trail of tears streamed down his face, and his mouth was open as if he was trying to offer the woman a silent apology. I grabbed his arm, snapping him out of the trance. "Lil bro, we gotta go. Now!"

"Bleeko, what the fuck, man?" his voice cracked up as he reached out for the little girl as if he could touch her from thirty feet away.

"Melly, we gotta go. It's not your fault. You didn't mean to do it. Come on before we can't get away from this bitch." I pulled his arm back towards the car and jumped inside.

I didn't hesitate to do a circle in my truck heading the opposite way. I could see the pain in Melly's eyes because he continued to look at the woman in the street until she was officially out of our sight. Swerving down Holly Street, I made my way down until we reached the end of the long block. I had to keep looking back in the rearview to make sure we weren't spotted because going back to Rice Street for another trial wasn't anywhere in my fucking schedule.

"Melly, give me yo gun, lil bro." I reached a hand out for it.

He hesitated to give it to me but obliged, and I already sensed the shit that just occurred was eating at his flesh. I placed both of our pistols into a plastic trash bag and sat it on the floorboard between my feet.

"Bleeko, what the fuck was that?" His eyes were piercing at me like I was the motherfucking enemy.

"What the fuck do you mean, what was it? A fucking shootout, nigga. I didn't have no control over that shit. I hope you ain't tryin to blame that on me?"

"It sounds more like you blaming it on yourself." He flashed an expression that made me dumb uncomfortable.

I laughed, knowing that I could easily snap, but instead, I played the role to see where lil bro's mind was at when I pulled up inside the Bankhead Transit Station. "Check this out. Go ahead and catch the train, ride out for a few hours before you try and come back on this side of town. I'll get rid of these guns and switch up cars before the police lock this shit down over here."

He sat still for a while like he was debating on going, but eventually opened the car door with aggression in his posture. Before he could close it, I let him know exactly where my mind was.

"Keep this shit quiet, Melly. I'll handle Lonnie's brother, but we don't need this shit going viral lil bro."

He never responded, but the look in his eyes said that he damn sure understood. Watching him close the door and jog quickly inside the train station, I placed the car in reverse and instantly thought about my first victim.

* * *

Five Points Transition Station-Underground Atlanta.
Thirty-five Minutes Later

My heart was still pounding profusely after I got off the train at the underground. The pain of seeing that woman holding her baby girl was eating at me like a motherfucker, and the guilt of possibly releasing that bullet from my gun is what killed me even more. My eyes still could still see the flashes like fireworks, the child's blood, a large hole pierced through the back. It was so traumatic that I froze. My arms wanted to console that woman and her seed so bad that I forgot my gun was just used to take the life of another man also. I knew Bleeko would get rid of the guns, but the question was who all saw what went down tonight. I hoped that Silent Avenue would remain home and firm on that foundation.

Easing my way through the Underground's glass doors, I took the escalator to the bottom floor. My eyes instantly examined the flatscreen that read: "Child Murdered in Shootout." That shit sent a massive surge of guilt down my flesh, and I quickly started to examine the people who were moving around me. I had to be sure that my name wasn't mentioned. My ears were trying to tune in over the loud clamor in the busy tunnel. I nearly bumped into four motherfuckers trying to reach the bottom floor until the words: "No suspects yet," flashed under the headlines. My mind pondered quickly to the hood. The store building, I knew for a fact that the cops were bound to head over for a review of the footage. My mind was racing every damn where, and I still had yet to call Kay-Kay to warn her about my troubles. I knew for a fact she would never trade on me or say nothing for nobody. She was my true Queen.

It was traffic moving two ways down the walkway, and I had to find a place to sit back, so I moved to the food court. I stopped at the pizza parlor ordering a small orange soda and slice of hot pepperoni. My stomach was turning knots, and I had to put something inside it before I puked from nausea that was slightly overtaking me. I usually didn't care about handling my business when it came to that gun play, but the little's girl's life was a casualty in the mix of whatever I was just involved in. That was a different type of emotion from ensuring another nigga caught one before me.

Taking a seat at a table, I sat the food in front of me and rubbed both hands across my face to calm the fuck down. I knew for a fact that I didn't have any beef, and before I allowed a man to claim my life for the cause of something Bleeko had done, I would handle his stupid ass first.

I held my head low for a while in slight disappointment for following around with this idiot, and just when I decided to take a bite of the pizza, a woman came and sat gently down at my table in front of me like we were about to share a meal. I looked up into her eyes, wondering if she had me mistaken for someone else, and was instantly stricken by her beauty.

Red lipstick was coating her luscious lips. Her hair was pulled back in a ponytail, and her dimples were flashing, showing off the gorgeous smile. The caramel skin she possessed was glowing to perfection. After gazing into her mesmerizing eyes for a good second, I realized that she was the fine Sista from Randy's barbershop that gave me her number a few days back. She was looking beyond good in her white Adidas tracksuit and slippers. The face she gave me was asking why in the fuck I didn't text her phone like she asked.

"Hey, it's good to see you again," she spoke sweetly to me.

I smiled, sitting the slice of pizza back in the box. "You too, ma. How did you just recognize me out of nowhere like that?"

"I asked you to text me," she responded, ignoring my question.

I sat back with a guilty face as if I was gonna think of a good answer to give back, but instead, I kept it real. "I'm sorry, baby girl, but I'm in a relationship. I meant to tell you the last time, but I didn't want to seem like I wasn't interested. You're a beautiful woman, but I would have to settle for a friendship, ma."

Her eyes were locked in on me like I was a first-class meal, but the expression she wore said differently. I watched her reach into a small Christian Dior handbag and scribbled something on a piece of paper before sliding it across the table to me.

"Please text my phone. It's important." I read the note that was jotted down with her number. By the time I raised my head to reply, she was walking off from the table as if we were never having that conversation. I didn't know what the hell was so important that she just couldn't say whatever it was in front of me. The shit that was on my mind at the time had me wallowing in my own pool of trouble, and I didn't have time to play the guessing game with this chick.

Taking her number, I slid it in my pocket and bit the pizza. Before I could process my second thought, my phone started to vibrate. The shit caught me off guard, and I sat there for a second as if the police had just been alerted on my identification. Pulling it out of my front pants pocket, I saw Kaycake flashing across the screen. Answering the call, I placed it up to my ear, being sure to stay aware of my surroundings. "Yeah?

"Melly? Oh my God, baby! Where are you? Have you seen what the hell is going on over here on this side of town?" she questioned me in a panic.

I knew that I couldn't just come out and tell her over the phone what just occurred, and I damn sure didn't need her flipping out on me either. How did you explain to your other half that you were possibly the one who took the life of a small child in the midst of trading bullets with some niggas I had nothing to do with?

"Yeah, I know. It's all over the news right now," I replied calmly, not trying to ruffle her nerves.

"A child was murdered down on Silent Avenue. It's like the entire media is down there right now. Where are you?"

"I'm safe. I'm not trying to do much talking over this phone right now, Kay-Kay. Just wait up for me, and I'll be home soon."

"Melly, you're scaring me!"

"Calm down because there is nothing to be scared about. I'm just having a few drinks with a friend on the other side of town. I'll be on my way back home in a few. I'm fine, ma," I tried to stress inside the line so she could end the back-and-forth conversation across the damn phone.

"Okay, baby." She exhaled in my ear.

Hanging up my phone, I sat still for about thirty more seconds before tearing it down through the food court. I wasn't about to stand still any longer, but I needed a little time to let the hood breathe before I made my way back. All I knew is one thing for sure; I wasn't trying to hear my name being plastered on the television screen across the globe for murdering that baby. Asking for forgiveness would only work with the man upstairs, but it also took changing the way I moved. It was literally gonna be my last time rocking with that nigga Bleeko. Whether shit turned out sour or good.

Chapter 8
Kay-Kay

As I stared around the unfamiliar home, I noticed that Christmas decorations were aligned against every wall as if the holiday just appeared in thin air. Not to mention, it was hot like the pit of hell, but it was in the middle of August. Four months away from December. I stared around at the mounted pictures on the walls and as I tried to make out the faces. The photographs seemed to become a blur. The lights that were just sparkling in my pupils shut off simultaneously, and I was now standing in a dark living room without a sound or person around me. The small little light over the Christmas tree was the only thing still glowing, and all I could make out was the numbers 626 across the holiday poster hanging behind it. The sound of a small grunt released in the air, causing my head to jerk around quickly. The flickering of light was coming from what appeared to be a kitchen, and my heart pounded profusely when I felt my feet move on their own, heading in that direction. It's like I wasn't in control of my own body. The closer I got to the spooky-looking area, the more I tried to stop my legs from moving forward. The lights were now flickering faster as if someone was purposely playing with the light switch. I tried to speak and scream out for Melly's name, but my lips felt tighter than two pieces of paper bounded with gorilla glue. Just as my feet were about to reach the entrance of the kitchen, the lights shut off, leaving me staring inside the dark space in fear. I heard another grunt, and that shit caused me to close my eyes, knowing that whatever was about to kill me had probably already gotten to my man before he could even get a chance to help me. I spotted the lights from the kitchen cut back on through my closed lids. When I opened my eyes, I shivered, praying that the lord could remove my sight from the horrific scene.

Blood was covering the kitchen floor. From the trash and chairs that were knocked over, you could tell there had been a scuffle, and the old lady who bled horribly from the face was bounded against the far corner wall. Her hands were tied behind her, and that's when I heard a small grunt release from her lips. My heart was pounding as if it would pop at any second, and that's when the scariest shit I've ever seen occur. The woman's body sat straight up from the floor, flashing me a creepy smile. Her head crooked to the side like she was trying to break her own neck before speaking, "All you need is love, and you ain't gotta beg me for my help, baby. You're loved."

Jumping out of my sleep, I grabbed ahold of my chest and looked around nervously. Melly was no longer lying beside me, and the alarm clock on our dresser read 6:01. I realized that I was in my own bed, and I didn't hesitate to climb out that bitch to make sure my legs didn't possess a demonic spirit like I was Emily Rose.

Stepping out into the hallway, I reached the living room, Where Melly sat on the couch staring at the Flat screen TV like it would surely disappear by morning. He looked like he hadn't gotten an ounce of sleep after making it home last night, and from the story, he told me. I know that his conscience was eating at him. Still, I refused to let him feel that he was alone in the situation, so I tried my best to console him as much as possible.

"Baby, why are you still up?" I wiped the corners of my eyes before taking a seat next to him.

"Because Kay-Kay, I got a feeling that somethin ain't right. I don't wanna panic, but at the same time, I can't just sit back as if I wasn't involved with that shooting." He rubbed his temples in distress.

Of course, I knew that a murder wasn't shit to be calm about, especially when it involved a baby, but it was always the same shit I stressed to Melly years before this even occurred. Bleeko was a selfish ass nigga, and his bullheaded ways could easily get him killed if Melly wasn't careful when being around that clown. In the past nine months, Bleeko's name had been mixed into everything from robbery, murder, drug dealing, and even shit that could make a man's brother turn his back without even looking back to say goodbye. It was even spookier because I was having these crazy-ass dreams back-to-back, and the signs were starting to eat at me. I felt like it was something my brain wanted to show me, but I just couldn't put it together.

I rubbed Melly's shoulder and placed a kiss on his cheek. "Baby, I'm never gonna grill you and say that I told you so, but don't weigh so much of this guilt on you. You're not the only person that was down there shooting. What gives you the thought that you're the one who did it?"

I waited for an answer, but I could see that he truly didn't know what to say. It was hard on him, especially when a daughter was all he stressed about having with me. Out of all the things he had been tied into, I'd never seen him so distraught. Even though I wanted to hold back my thoughts, I didn't know if it would be an assistance to him in some kind of way.

"Baby, lately, I've been having a lot of bad dreams since Bleeko has been closer to you. The same way your dreams have been getting out of hand while you're sleeping. Don't you think that's kind of weird?"

He instantly huffed like I was thinking too damn hard, and I could see that he didn't even want to speak on that topic.

"They're dreams, Kay-Kay. Some will be bad, some good. That doesn't have anything to do with the way I move out here, baby." He looked at me with a nonchalant expression.

"But what if they're not just dreams, Melly? What if it's really signs that we need to be paying attention to?"

He put a fist on his chin, staring at me like I was going crazy. "Like what, Kay-Kay? Like psychic signs?"

"Exactly."

Shaking his head, he stood up and exhaled deeply. "Baby, I understand that you're worried or even the fact that you don't like me hanging with this nigga, Bleeko, but that shit you speaking on now is just absurd. This is some serious shit. Maybe I do need to try the religion thing. Maybe I do need to get the hell away from Silent Avenue. I don't know. I'm just trying to focus on this problem I have on my hands, and we can worry about your hypothesis of being a mind reader later on cause it's not gonna help me in no kind of way. I'm gonna go grab a shower and get ready to drop you off at work. You might need to try and get you thirty more minutes of rest because I don't need both of us going crazy," he said to me before walking off as if my opinion didn't mean shit.

I started to throw the remote to hit his hardheaded ass in the back of his skull so he could try and listen to somebody else besides his own damn conscience. Melly was my king, true enough, but he had a nasty way of dealing with his problems when his feelings got involved. He would shut me out, and that only barricaded us further away from each other when I tried to help.

As I sat in my thoughts, my eyes gazed at the television. The replay of yesterday's lottery numbers was being broadcasted, and my mouth flopped open like a stanky bitch who needed some cock when I saw the number 626 fall across the screen. I nearly shitted on myself, thinking that God was trying to punish me for some reason. I immediately felt like somebody was about to jump out and get my ass in my own crib. Before I had a chance to run into the dead granny or anymore bloody Christmas houses, I made my way quickly to the bathroom with my ass and titties jiggling everywhere just to make it to Melly. My heart was pumping harder than a runaway train, and that was the first time that I thought someone was about to kill me in the bounds of my own home. I was so scared that I had to go and suck on my baby just to make sure he wasn't gonna be absent if this demon popped back up to do me in. It was something weird going on around us, and I wasn't gonna stop until Melly saw the shit that was playing through my eyes because whatever it was didn't have any intentions of leaving us alone until its presence was clear.

* * *

Atlanta Police Department
Zone One Precinct
Detective Solomon

After getting to work early this morning, it was a long briefing about the murder of the little girl, Denaisha, on my block. This Silent Avenue bullshit was unreal. It took the life of a precious soul. The pain this woman suffered with is a feeling that I wouldn't wish on my worst enemy. Right after the meeting was dismissed, my boss man, Captain Baxter, called me in for a private sit down in his office. Part of me already knew what it was about, but I still chose to keep my mouth shut until he explained what the hell was going on.

Stepping into his office, I took a seat and watched him closely as he finished up the phone conversation that he was having. The potency of his tone told me that he was still hot about the Investigators climbing up our precinct's tail.

The bureau wanted answers. Fast ones. I was the leading officer on the scene of her murder, and I still had not one conclusive piece of evidence to lock anybody behind bars, which is the reason I was probably about to be grilled harder than fresh skinned mackerel out of the bay.

Baxter ended his call, leaning back in his seat with an unsettling grumble. I could tell that he was masking his anger with me. I was a good detective, a damn good one, but not enough to be excused from the life of little Denaisha.

"Explain to me one thing, Mr. June. You've been a detective for my force quite a while, and you've done work that can never be replaced by anyone in this precinct. I'm a witness to that. But why is it when I hear the names of your associates on my desk that I never see them entering my precinct in a pair of cuffs?"

"Why can't you just call me Solomon, sir. I hate that name." I exhaled, knowing exactly where this conversation was about to lead.

"I'm quite sure that a lot of law-abiding citizens do. Don't give me a question with a question, son." He was pointing his index finger sturdily to show his seriousness. His jawbones would always rise, and clench indicating when he was pissed, beyond furious to be exact.

"I was the first on the scene, sir. I followed all proper procedures, questioned nearby residences, stores, even the homeless people strolling around on the fix."

"And what's next?" Baxter replied as if I were missing a large chapter of an Edward Bunker novel.

My mind had to decrease on the sarcasm I was prepared to deliver; he was still my boss, an arrogant prick by heart, but a fair one. I blew out a deep breather catching my asshole side before it seeped through the pores of my skin like a batch of pure Columbia's finest. "And I came up with nothing, sir," I answered truthfully.

"My point, Solomon," he fired back sarcastically, dragging my first name out as if he would get it wrong. "Nothing in the past six months has been arrested in your area besides the small peddlers and soliciting junkies who can't even purchase a single loosie from the neighborhood's bootlegger. I'm lost for words right now." He shook his head in disbelief as if I was the trigger man.

"Captain Baxter, I'm pushing the clock nonstop today until I receive some answers about this little girl's death. You know, just like I do, I won't rest until it's handled. I'm not asking you to give me a pat on the back, sir, just time. I need more time to take every son of a bitch down that even pondered on placing their hands around the handle of a gun that night. If that means Brandon being brought in for questioning, so be it. He's not off-limits. And just to be clear, sir, with all respect, that bastard is no associate of mine, let alone any kin. I wouldn't claim that motherfucker if my mama had a chance to be saved off her deathbed," I cursed with slang dripping off my tongue.

Baxter could see the frustration that was bulging through my eyes, the plea for a little patience on being the detective that he knew I could be. It was enough pain dealing with the loathing mother of the slain child, and a promise had already been made to her that night about her killers being brought to justice, even if that closure meant a bullet from my handgun. He exhaled deeply. Placing on his reading glasses, he removed a file from his top desk. It was photos and a brief summary of whatever information he gathered from an unreliable source.

"Last night, graveyard shift picked up a woman preparing to turn a trick with a man who happened to be in possession of a kilo of heroin. The little princess obviously heard the charges that were about to be stacked against her new federal case and sang like a yellow canary. Apparently, she had a few more things to offer the force. She claims to know who pulled the Hunter Hills murder. She also claims if we get the hands on these two individuals, they might explain just what happened with this child losing her life," he explained before tossing the papers to me.

Of course, my mind knew that line suspect would be Bleeko's peanut brain ass. His mugshot alone said I wasn't shit and please throw me in a fucking cell, captivating me for eternity. The second was a shocker. Never seen the young man too often, and if I did, he was carrying himself like a gentleman. I glared down at his picture before turning it around for Baxter's eyes to view. "This guy, I know him. Meltavious Hicks. He's not even a kid like that. His father was Franklin."

Baxter's eyebrows arched as if I was reading him a midnight child's story, the one where the happy ending is always crummy, fictional work at its best.

"Seems like you have a bundle of relative troubles on your hand, Solomon. I'm never the one to press, trust I could get tighter than an Allen wrench cracking a bolt, but these thugs that's running my streets, feeling as if the world belongs to them like the rerun of Mr. Tony Montana, you need to shut it down pronto. I don't need another episode like Kato's spilling in my city. If you hate your last name so bad, bury it alive." He leaned in closer with his last few words, and the emphasis made me slightly agitated, "And be sure it never surfaces again."

"Understood," I bit my tongue from telling the hog body bastard to shove this badge up his ass before standing to my feet. Instead, I took the lick on the chin like a champ and made my way out of his office.

Leaving the precinct, I climbed behind the wheel of my cruiser, glancing at the picture of my sweet mama for some of that warm guidance. I know that I kept a clean suit and straight tie when it came to the way I was presenting myself in these streets as a youngster coming up. That was all because of the way she raised me after I was adopted into her home. Now that I was older, I've found myself fighting with the same individuals who shared more of a past with me than the loveable citizens knew. It was time to fight fire with fire. The only way to draw a hoodlum out of the hood was to become the hoodlum. It was a crucial game to place my coins against, but for the sake of Mama June, I wasn't about to fail her now.

Chapter 9
Cascade Road
Melly

After dropping Kay-Kay off at the Small Smiles Center for work, I decided to go out and find something productive to do so that I could free my mind of all the dirty thoughts I'd been having. Remorse was in my spirit, so much that I wanted to find that nigga Lonnie my damn self, deliver him to Denaisha's mother, letting her pull the trigger from a gun at the same time as me. These clowns were so stuck on the miniature beefing in the streets that they never pondered on the innocent people that could easily be drowned in the waves of their self-destructive decisions. It was chaos at its finest, around the hood, and I was planning on making my transition out of this bitch after giving that child's mother some relief. It's like I wanted to scream for God, asking him to take these problems away, though it didn't work that easy.

Stopping at the nearby Texaco gas station, I grabbed myself a hot cup of black beaned Maxwell coffee, a Five-Hour Energy to kick away my sleepiness, and a pack of chewing gum. As I headed out of the door, not paying attention to the man in front of me, I bumped directly into him, knocking all of his things to the ground. The entire coffee nearly spilled on my shirt, forcing me to bite on my lip from the slight burning sensation that caressed my skin through the thin T-shirt.

"Damn, man. I'm sorry, bruh. I wasn't paying attention," I offered an apology while helping him pick up the books and papers that were scattered on the ground.

"Ah man, It's all good, young brother. It was an accident," he replied while scrapping up a few of the items himself.

My eyes landed on the beautiful leather Noble Quran laying on its side, causing me to reach for it before standing to my feet. I looked the older cat in his eyes and realized that he was a Muslim man. His eyebrows were bushy and formed a unibrow. His beard was fully grey, and a black kufi was pulled down tightly over his head. His smile was welcoming and seemed as if he wasn't never the type to grow angry for any cause.

"This is a beautiful Quran you got here, bro. That thing looks like it cost a grip." I rubbed the front cover before handing it over.

He chuckled and shook his head. "Nah, lil bro. It's the love of Allah, and that doesn't cost a thing. Do you know anything about the Quran?" he asked with an inquisitive face.

"Me? Oh nooo. Man, I barely know anything about God, period. Unfortunately, I wasn't raised around that great character and holy people, like most." I shrugged, really lost for how to reply, so I just kept it gutta.

Pushing the glasses up on his face closer to his eyes, he placed the religious book back in my hands.

"Do me a favor. Turn to Surah 6 Al-Anam. Iyat 140. It should be on page 149," he said calmly.

Of course, not having any understanding of the Qur'an, I opened it from the front. He gently grabbed it from my palms, flipping it to its backside.

"You need to read from the back, brother. Right to left." A smile was on his face, realizing that I was embarrassed.

"Okay," I uttered before turning to the page he instructed me to. Once I found my designated chapter and line, I began to read. "Indeed, lost are they who have killed their children foolishly without knowledge and have forbidden that which Allah has provided for them, inventing a lie against Allah. They have indeed gone astray and were not guided," I finished, looking up at him with a clueless ass face.

"I give you that Iyat to say, many people have led their children down wrong paths and haven't conveyed his message. Whether from not having knowledge or having it, but not acting upon it, no man can lead anyone astray that Allah chooses to guide. You can learn any religion if you are dedicated to trying."

"True." I nodded in agreement. "But you know how it be when you're raised in these streets. I've had friends take care of me more than family. That's where my trust got placed. How can you cross out the same people who helped you eat in this world? Never seem like it came from God then, and what makes your religion so good, over all others. How do I know I shouldn't be a Buddhist or a Christian?" I shot back, thinking that he was trying to be smart.

"Allah stated in the Quran that if you place your trust in man, surely you will fail. He's the creator, the giver of security, and controller of life and death. He has preordained everything that has taken place in this world, from the beginning to this exact moment that you're standing in front of me right now. Ask your friend who gives you these so-called blessings to get you into paradise. Do you feel that he can pull it off, or do you have to give your life to the supreme being to ensure that your darkest sins are forgiven and forgotten? Islam is the true religion because we believe in one God. The only God, brother," he explained thoroughly, forcing me to listen closely.

Out of my whole life, as far back as I can remember, no one had ever broken something down so quickly and simply to me. The part about forgiveness is what really grasped my attention. Over the past twenty hours, the only thing that I visioned or thought about was that sweet and innocent baby. I needed her forgiveness, her blessing, to know that I didn't have to worry myself with guilt for being around the idiot Bleeko at the wrong time. A simple meet-up to have fun at a club turned the world upside down, with one of the most tragic incidents that were still being broadcasted on every news station as I looked at the elder Muslim standing in front of me waiting patiently for a reply. I got a strange feeling in my gut that his guidance would surely help me if I wanted to make a change, at least to start trying.

"How long do you think it would take me to learn about your religion if I was interested?" I folded my arms curiously.

"You could never have enough time on this earth to learn it all, but starting now would make it easier." He grinned excitedly.

* * *

Bleeko

After watching the sun come up this morning, I decided to head out early in order to catch my first victim that was now on my shit list. The block was doing more than popping guns cause the word around Atlanta was that I had the streets on fire with the bodies that were now falling drastically on the westside. Now it was known to me that someone's lips were sealing my fate at that exact moment, ready to take me under the prison 'til my last fucking days crept up on me on this earth.

The Citgo gas station was barely crowded, and it made it quite easy to spot Latoya's nasty ass sashaying through the parking lot of the corner store looking like a Beverly Hills hooker from *Pretty Woman*. I could see her big ass pupils moving around widely as if they were begging for sleep. It didn't take long before a trick play pulled in on her. From the way she leaned down in his passenger window, he either was waving a sack of dope or some crispy bills because it was the only way she was pulling down them dirty ass tights that she clearly wore twice out of the week.

I watched her climb in the front seat of the pussy purchaser's whip and pull right behind the building. I didn't know if the bitch peeped me out across the street and flagged down the first car she saw, or if this was just my lucky day to catch this hoe down bad without making a scene. Back then, when my brother Kato was alive, he would've emptied the clip in LaToya, sunup, or down. His business and gangsta savvy allowed me to soak up his routines and implement them smoothly. My brain told me to move when I noticed the car didn't appear from the other side of the store to exit the lot. I didn't see too much traffic and letting this moment slip was tossed out of the window when she decided to stick something in her mouth, besides that toothbrush with a dab of Colgate.

Pulling my truck across the street into the Citgo, I drove calmly to the back. The small champagne sedan was parked, and only his head could be seen through the dirty rear window, which means that Latoya must have been busy down low with a mouth full of beef frank.

Killing my engine, I grabbed the silenced .9mm pistol from under my seat and jumped out before I second-guessed what I was about to do. Being sure not to catch a bullet from whoever was sitting in the car with her, I moved around to his side first and snatched the driver's door open.

Whack!

He was so busy getting some morning top that he barely could move until my gun collided with his nose, shattering his shit.

"Fuckkk!" He hunched over with a hand held out as if I didn't have to swing again.

Latoya's eyes started to drain with all life when she noticed that I was the one interrupting her twenty-dollar booty call. Before I could even reach across him to grab that bitch by the hair, she jumped out from the other side, heading deeper into the pathway that sat directly behind the gas station.

Grabbing the old man's keys, I quickly tossed them into a large pile of trash before taking off behind Latoya. The bitch was so high that I didn't even have to run. I paced myself a little bit faster after I watched her squeeze through a hole in the fence that led to the back of Bethune Elementary. I moved hastily through the steel wires, and when I crossed to the other side, I raised my gun, firing one shot.

Pwwt!

I watched her fall to the concrete as my bullet found a home, blowing off a chunk of her right leg.

I moved slowly over to her, being sure to catch my breath for what I needed to say before she left the world for good. She slid across the concrete, blood forming a trail beneath her, as she tried to think of a way to get past me with her life. Tears were streaming down Latoya's face when I finally stood over with my gun aimed down at her face.

"Bl-Bleek-o, please. I don't deserve this. I didn't say, anything daddy, I swear," she lied before I could even get a chance to speak.

I was kneeling down in front of her, and a smile formed on my face. I always loved when a motherfucker told on themselves. In a way, it made my job a tad bit easier. I didn't have to suffer with the regret of taking another's life, neither did I have to worry about the gossip of my actions being on the airwave.

"You messed up, Toya. It's either you or me, and I don't plan on going nowhere for a long time," I stressed to let her know that today would be our last chat.

Before she could even utter another lie, I removed the small pocketknife from my hoodie and slit her throat from ear to ear. Her arms flung around in a frantic as the dark blood rushed down her shirt and black tights. Aiming my gun, I placed one slug to the side of her temple and watched her chest heave in for the last time. A puddle of piss formed underneath her, and the relief of me keeping my freedom was starting to look much better.

Sliding the gun back on my hip, I grabbed Latoya by the armpits, dragging her near the large green dumpster. Resting her body against the side of it, I began to pile a few garbage bags around her to conceal the body. I didn't need her being spotted by anyone, and the abandoned school gave me a good time limit on her being found.

Making my way back through the cut, I proceeded to my truck, got in, and pulled off as if I just stopped for a quick fill-up. My mind was running faster than an engine, but I was still focused on what needed to be done. I had three more people to deal with, and until then, I was showing the city exactly why Bleeko was a name that you didn't want to mention.

Chris Green

Chapter 10
Melly

It was going on three in the afternoon by the time I finished my religious prep with the Muslim brother, Muhammad. I had to admit, I was never down with jumping into something blindly, but the facts and authenticity of the Quran made me ponder on actually converting. I still was cautious. Who wouldn't be? In the end, I knew changing for the better would only bring me to a certain form of peace, and Kay-Kay's parents some relief that I wasn't about to crash my baby out with any nonsense.

The busy streets of Silent Avenue were pumping like the usual afternoon, and the thought of my cousin Nita crossed my mind as I passed down Ashby. Making a quick turn on Troy Street, I slowed my car down once I reached the small set of apartments that looked as if they were going to collapse at any second. Not too many of my family members were left around the city, and the closest person I had left to me was my cousin Nita. She was my Auntie Fema's daughter. She was seven years older than me and never had too much of a reason to smile after losing her mama twenty years back, along with my mother, Felicia, and father, Franklin. Nina was nearly placed into every mental institution, psychiatrist, and physical therapist to try and help with her pain of dealing with the steady drug battles and losses. It was hard for a lot of us, but Nita was weaker than a few of my family members. It was only a handful of us still standing around Georgia, but I've always held my head high like nothing could stop me from being somebody.

Hopping out of the driver's seat of my car, I strolled up the pathway that led to her front door. I only tapped on the entrance a few times. No one wouldn't want to force her to think they were coming with bad intentions. Nita could get wild with that .38 revolver when she hadn't been around anyone close in a while, and I damn sure didn't have time for one of her episodes today after the wreckage already possessed on my brain.

After a few seconds of silence and listening to the chattering civilians that moved about through the complex, I heard the lock shift and opened. The door came ajar, and Nita stuck her head out like a suspicious neighbor catching a break-in.

She whispered, "Why you knockin' on de'doe like a damn officer, Melly? I'm six months past due on my rent, and you know them eviction people riding through on the regular." She stepped to the side, allowing me to cross her threshold.

The smell of overcooked salmon and grits were lingering in the air. The sounds of my baby cousin, Maliyah, crying forced me to look around the living room until I spotted her flopping around the floor on her belly as if she desired to be picked up at that moment. Of course, I wasted no time scooping her up, placing a few big kisses on her chubby little cheek.

"So, what brings you this way, Meltavious? It's been almost two months since you last checked in on me. Let me find out you've actually made some time to bond with the last of the lil family we do have." Nita smirked before taking her seat back on the half-decent couch.

I tickled Maliyah on the bottom of her toes before matching my cousin's curious gaze.

"It's not like that, Nita. Kay-Kay and I have been working pretty hard to establish something for our future. You know I'm barely in good graces with her dad, but I'm going to the moon and back about mine," I replied before tickling Maliyah's belly with a finger.

Nita smacked her lips like my statement wasn't important.

"Melly, how you know that girl really ready for that? If you ask me, I'd say stay away from dem folks and hold on to the last of this little bloodline we got left. We're falling apart with the years that's passing by, and I'm not down with supporting you on moving away like our last name just don't matter no mo." Her face balled up, just speaking about the matter.

It was a waste of time even putting up an argument because I was damn sure gonna lose. I wanted what was best for little Maliyah, and that was my Cousin Nita going to rehab for a while in order to gain her strength to raise a seed properly. Every time I slid through her neck of the woods, she was either asking for money or chewing me out about not allowing her to do as she please if I wasn't providing for her. In a way, I understood her reasoning, but that shit didn't matter when you cared about your relatives for real.

Sitting Maliyah inside of her jumper, I took a seat next to Nita and placed a hand on her shoulder. "Listen, cuz, this might not be what you want to hear, but I'm actually trying to do something with my life. I don't just want to be known as the college dropout that went drug dealer because of money troubles. Just because I make money from this doesn't mean that I want you blazing up the same shit like my wrongs make you right. I wanna see you make it out of here the same way I want to, Nita." I looked square into her eyes to show my sincerity.

"Nigga, I smoke crack. My bills are so overdue that I've earned the first award for being the deepest in the negative, and I haven't had a job since Dixie Land, my tenth-grade school year. What the fuck do I care about leaving the damn ghetto?" She shrugged while picking through the cigarette butts in her ashtray.

I felt bad hearing her speak so harshly about her life while having my baby cousin underneath her as a guardian. You could only push so far for someone that didn't care for themselves, but did that actually apply for family who you felt had no hope. As bad as I wanted to snatch her up and force the change upon Nita, it didn't mean that it would be effective. Her world was shattered decades ago and trying to show her happiness was still out there, was like arguing with the devil about sins not being accepted as good deeds. All I could do was offer my words of encouragement where I saw fit and give all the help for the strength of my blood Maliyah.

Standing up, I pulled a few twenties from my pocket and placed them into her palm. The look in her eyes told me where it was about to go, but the effort for trying to assist her was all that rested in my mind at the moment. "If you're smart, you'll buy Maliyah the stuff she needs. Nothing is more important than family, right?" I questioned, tilting my head, my pupils still trained on her.

"Melly, my family was taken away from me. I've given my entire life to being a better person, as they call it. Some things just aren't meant to change, and everybody ain't meant to make it. Joe Boy ain't stressing; wherever he is, I can bet ya that. He may be fooling everybody else, but not me."

Nita wiggled her finger at me as if I were a disobeying child, but I was clueless about all the collage of words and emotions that poured from her. I didn't know who the hell Joe Boy was and damn sure wasn't trying to understand the complication. Her rent was nearly half of what the usual people in the upper complex paid, and the lack of her ambition to do better was killing her softly like a Lauryn Hill song. It hurts to watch family suffer, to experience an unbearable pain that one wouldn't want to wish on their worst enemy. I loved Nita, but the strength would have to come from within before I was ever able to put forth the effort to pull her from the destruction.

Placing a kiss on her cheek, I handed her a hundred dollars and smiled.

"Nita, we all have trials and tribulations, cuzo. We just have to remain steadfast with our faith. A friend of mine told me that today," I offered the motivational tidbit that I was able to lock in on a few hours ago while heading for the door.

She turned up her nose at the statement, but her reply was much better than I expected.

"I guess God might work in a little patience for me one day. That's a step I haven't been pressured to take yet, Melly. Maybe it'll be soon, though, ya know."

A small smile crept upon my face knowing that my big cousin, Nita, was somewhere still inside the lost woman that stood in front of me. I knew that she could be strong during some real ass times, but I couldn't help but see a different destiny for her life if she didn't take the opportunity to stand on her own as a black queen should.

"Just focus, baby girl. You got this," I assured, trying to leave her with a tad of inspiration to spark the flame in her soul.

Stepping out on the front porch, I strolled back down the driveway. My movements paused when I noticed a few guys posted in front of my whip like they were waiting on me to arrive. I could see Trev and Dunk also, but their hands were occupied with bottles of tequila and blunts as if it were just another day. By the time I got closer, I had noticed that they all clearly had guns attached to their waist, but I didn't sweat it for a second.

"Melly, what's the word around the hood?" Dunk asked with his thick deep voice. His beard was long like Pastor Troy, and his face always formed a mug when he looked down at me. Still, there was no intimidation whatsoever.

Tossing the boys a deuce, I smirked at Dunk. "Heyy, man, you know what the hood says. Don't speak on shit you don't know about. I'm a whole lame out chea," I teased like I really wasn't on point.

His eyes flared with anger, and the bitch ass double-mint crash dummy twins behind him were already clutching on their pistol handles like crazy.

"Shitttt nigga. If you a lame, why you ain't paying to be around here on this corner? This Troy Street, not Simpson or Silent Ave, as you call it. You don't mean nuthin down here, fool," he spat with a more vigor tone.

"You're absolutely right, bruh," I complied, immediately knowing that I didn't have too much of an advantage. I had my registered gun in the holster under my shoulder. I damn sure wasn't about to try and reach in my jacket and become an air balloon before I even got a chance to defend myself. Sucking up my pride, I shook my head lowly, wanting so desperately to bite the bait. Instead, I held my hands up in peace. "I'm nobody, bro. I'm leaving immediately, and I don't need any trouble."

"Sounds like a good plan." He shooed me off like I was a bitch or something.

Trev and Dunk didn't say shit, which kind of threw me for a loop. We've never had beef in the streets, and on the strength of Bleeko, they've always ridden when the signs of trouble were seen. I could tell from the way they just stood there that it was obviously some bad energy in the air.

"Ah, Melly," Dunk called out to me before I jumped in my driver seat.

"Yo?"

"Be careful, my nigga, the streets saying the Hunter Hill's murder is your work. I would advise you to watch who you hanging with 'cause you might be up for a criminal case soon,

bro. That's just a warning before you bump ya head again."
He shrugged as if it really didn't matter what I chose to do.

Taking that little sign with silence, I tossed up a thumb and
didn't hesitate to press the gas when I climbed behind the
wheel. Being sure to keep my eyes on the rearview to make
sure I wasn't set up to be ambushed. I made my way out of the
suffocating street and turned back down Ashby. It's like my
day was really going okay until I crossed sides back over to
the hood. As soon as my bumper hit the edge of the corner
where the yellow store sat, an Atlanta police cruiser blue
lighted me and swerved in front of me like I was being tracked
for a bank robbery.

Two suited men stepped from their car with their guns
drawn.

"Get the fuck out of the car. Now! I wanna see your fucking hands, or you'll be wishing you were dead when I shoot
ya," the white officer made clear before they could even walk
close to the driver's door.

Holding my composure, I placed my hands on the steering
wheel and exhaled as a bald black male made his way towards
my side. His face didn't say Mr. Asshole, but there was never
a dull day with a black cop.

His fingers tapped my window gently, and I didn't hesitate
to roll it down.

"Is there a problem, officer?" I gazed up into the suspicious ass black sunglasses he was wearing.

"Mr. Hicks. Damn, it's crazy that I run into you after all
this chaos that's been going around the block. Now, is that a
coincidence or what?" He removed them and eyed me with
curiosity.

Brushing off his remark, I huffed, "Unfortunately, I'm not
the cause of it, so I wouldn't know, sir."

"Oh, but I thank you is, son. See, I know your kind. Franklin was your dad. A good man. One I respected, but I can't say that you're moving the correct way he was, at least for what I did know about him. We've had a murder around your way, and it seems that your entourage is showing up as suspects. Is this the trip you're trying to take?" he questioned with authority.

I didn't answer. Instead, I looked on to see what his next request would be.

"ID and registration," he demanded like his attitude would make me comply more. I still was sure to follow all rules in case they tried to free pick me as the black man bucking and forced to be shot. It was a dirty game.

I watched as he handed my info over to the eager white officer, who looked more disappointed that he didn't get a chance to shoot. He gave him the order to go and run my name, and he quickly dispersed, leaving the two of us alone. The sight of his frown let me know that I was probably in for a trip to the county if the pig wasn't smelling my vibe or if I had a warrant for anything.

The routine was quite simple. Comply or get yo black ass shot. Obey and still possibly get yo ass shot. I didn't want to be their weekday news report, so I just tried to stay quiet.

"I'm gonna explain something to you, Mr. Hicks. Silent Avenue is my street. Zone 1 is my area, and when it comes to lives being lost in my hood, I want to know who the hell is big enough to go against me when I'm known for trying to die about this law. Word of advice. Watch your company because one of these days, you might wake up in a jail cell with a snitching ass codefendant building a case fatter than Biggie Smalls on you."

"Unfortunately, I'm not in these streets, sir. I'm only living here, so I wouldn't have any clue about what you mean." I brushed him off with a calm posture.

"Oh yeah? You know that's funny, being that your name is sliding up around the Hunter Hill's murder, Hicks. You're being watched, and I suggest you play your cards smooth, or you will find out just exactly how much it takes to get caught in a knot with me, son. Take heed! I'm watching everything, and I'm not coming easy when it has something to do with my citizens. I pray you understand that. Do yourself a favor and be quiet for me." He waved me off.

Huffing in frustration, the pit of my stomach bubbled after hearing the officer mention a homicide. I didn't want to leave Kay-Kay and everyone else, neither did I need to be on the cops' radar when I was already doing enough wrong. My pupils rotated to the side mirror. The white officer was making his way back towards my car, but his face was unreadable. One thing was for sure, if it were bad news, my chance of marrying Kay-Kay and ending the memory of my family's downfall would be over.

"He's clean. Looks like a college student from what I've seen. Nothing but a few aggravated assaults at the school," he spoke dryly as if that was a shocker.

Officer Solomon grabbed my driver's info, tossing it back through my window with a shitty face. Placing his glasses back closer to his face, his fingers formed the shape of a gun, pointing at me straighter than a bow and arrow. Eyes piercing at mines, silently telling me that I was dead if another slip-up happened to occur.

"Have a good day, Mr. Hicks," Solomon said with distaste before nodding, sliding back to his cruiser quicker than he stopped me. The stop was obviously illegal, but I didn't have time to wonder about it. I was more grateful to walk away without being thrown in those cuffs. The thought of what he mentioned processed through my head as I watched them pull back off into the moving traffic like they were never there. I wasn't planning on going to the slammer no time soon or having a codefendant talking about shit because the friendship roles with these fake-ass street gangstas were over.

A thought crossed my mind as I swerved off the opposite way and headed for the Southside of Atlanta. I knew one person that could tell me anything. I needed to know if my name was really hot in the city. The real info I needed to put some pieces together and prepare for my exit out this stupid-ass profiled environment for good.

* * *

It didn't take more than twenty minutes before I found myself pulling up in front of Bleeko's safe house, where I last saw his sister Fanta. I wasn't here for her brother, and I prayed that I didn't have to run across his path for any interaction period. The driveway was empty besides a cream-colored Jeep Rubicon that sat parked on the side of the home.

Jumping out of the car, I headed for the front door and knocked when I reached the front porch. I waited for a second to see if anyone would answer, but I didn't want to look obvious with knocking on this idiot's dope spot while the sun was still high. At the moment, I was really out of choices. The locks adjusting forced my posture to tighten up, and once the door came open, Fanta stepped from behind it with a pair of low-cut shorts and fitted Tomboy shirt. Her body was begging for attention, and the makeup she wore made her appearance even more attractive. I had to look her over a few times before actually opening my mouth.

"Melly, what yo fine black ass doing over here? Bleeko's ass ain't here and ain't welcome back over her according to my people. I guess that left me in charge. You tryna fuck for some money" She eyed me up and down as her legs shifted to one side, showing her curvy butt and thighs in the doorway.

"Hey, Fanta. I didn't come for Bleeko; I came for you."

I watched her eyes glitter with excitement and quickly rained a storm on her silly ass parade.

"But it's not like I came for that type of stuff. I just needed to ask you a question or two," I corrected myself before she got out of hand.

"Step in," she said as more of a demand than a request.

I tried my best to scoot past her when I reached the door, but her breast and hard nipples rubbed against my chest and arms. I waited as she applied the locks and turned to face me, tongue running across her top lip like a feast was about to be prepared.

"Uhh, good morning." I backed up a tad when Fanta pulled into my personal space. Her fingers danced across my chest happily. "I know you're connected with some people in the streets. Out of town and in. It seems like my name is going around about a murder. Do you know anything or heard something about that? I could make it worth your while, if necessary," I added with a straight face.

"Oh, ah! That depends on what you tryna come off of, big daddy?" Her hand dipped down, caressing her crotch for a few seconds. It took my distraction lightly, but the thought of what was at hand quickly jumped back into my vision.

"That depends on what I get to find out," I shot back, not trying to play games with her mental health ass.

Her smile said that she was devising something much different inside of her brain than a nice payday, but I had to be sure in case she could really help me with something valuable.

Fanta folded her arms, exhaling, "Melly, I'm all the way on the south side of the A, and I've probably heard about your entire life story through the airwaves. You're like a celebrity in your hood, and we all know that celebrities get it first in the streets, love."

"What do you mean?" I asked, not really understanding what she was saying.

Her eyes batted at me flirtatiously, with a freaky smile. "Boy, Bleeko is trying to get the heat off his ass and tossed it on you. We all know he was beefing with that idiot at the Hunter Hill's store, and yo ass was moving right beside him like you had the pressure too. Now that shit has crumbled and started to come out; he's sitting the platter in your lap."

"Sit the platter in my lap?" I repeated slowly. "Like throwing this shit on me? Is that what you mean?" I stepped closer to make sure I wasn't hearing shit.

Fanta shrugged her shoulders with a nod and began to shed her clothes right in front of me. Her thick, black skin glowed as she stood naked, cupping her breast into her hands. She did a full spin, showing off her round apple booty, gently rocking it back and forth.

"Fanta put your clothes back on." I turned my head from all the goodies that were standing in front of me.

"Nah, Melly. Yo punk black ass got yo little info, and now I want some pickle. We can do this shit the easy or the hard way." Her braids swung around like she was ready to punch me out about the shit God placed into my pants. I didn't want to turn her against me, especially after the shit she just told me. I didn't feel comfortable doing anything that made me feel like I was stepping out on Kay-Kay, but I was refusing to leave her in the world alone because of my mistakes. I was willing to do whatever possible to keep my family. Even it meant pushing down on Bleeko myself.

"Get yo ass in that bedroom. I raised a hand, slamming a hard right hand across her soft butt.

"Ssss, shit, daddy!" Fanta bit her lips in anticipation.

"Don't keep me waiting too long." She moved seductively towards the hallway. After I watched her disappear into the back, my mind instantly went into think mode. Heading for the refrigerator, I opened it and scanned the inside for a second. My eyes rotated down to the vegetable bin and lit up with a golden idea when I spotted what I needed. Reaching down, I picked up a large cucumber and stuffed it down inside my pants. Trailing through the house, back to Fanta's room, I tapped lightly on her door before walking in. She was laid back against her headboard, stuffing two fingers inside the kitty like reaching for spare change under the couch.

"Is it okay if I hit the lights and close the curtains?" I asked, removing my shirt like I was ready to pound some shit to sleep.

"Oh, you like it in the dark, huh? It's cool." She grinned at me eagerly.

"Yea, you're in for a big surprise," I mumbled truthfully, thinking about the cold vegetable in my pants before dimming out the room.

Chapter 11
Kay-Kay

My day was already moving like a turtle's ass, and I was just finishing with my last child appointment for today. The small smiles center was busy earlier and being short of staff for today had us all moving hastily around the workplace. My co-worker, Christy, was giving all the assistance that she could, but her fat ass was only able to do so much. Once I cleared my office and station. I headed to the main desk of the clinic. By the time I reached the front. I watched as Christy practically ran through the entrance, locking the double doors behind her.

"What's wrong?"

"Get back! Go to the back!" she stressed with worry written on her face.

The bitch scared me immediately, and I didn't wait to haul ass towards a clinic room and rush in. Christy was right behind me like a dog's tail. Shaking like a leaf, she slammed the door behind us and looked back at me with fear glowing in her eyes.

"Kay-Kay, there's two guys with guns asking about you in the front. They didn't look too happy either." She was breathing heavily while trying to explain.

"What? Nobody knows where I work but Melly and my immediate family Christy. What did they say?"

"They grabbed me by the arm and asked if Kay-Kay, Melly's girlfriend, was working today."

"Okay bitch, and what did you say?" I was ready to panic, feeling like she just offered me to the slaughter. It was hard to believe something another bitch said if you weren't there to verify that shit ya damn self. For all I knew, Booty-man Craig from the Creek was probably searching for my ass.

"Kay-Kay, those guys looked like they were trying to hurt you, and I'm not talking long stroking hurt. I mean, bullet to the head hurt." She twiddled with her fingers like I was gonna have to give up my life for her or some shit.

Peeking my head out of the office door, I glared down the small hall at the entrance to see if I spotted these mystery guys lurking around so I could try and get a face visual. Just when I thought this bitch might have been high on something. The nasty face of an ugly, skinny motherfucker started peeping in like he was on a mission. A big ass gun was in one of his hands, and he damn sho looked like he would rape someone if he got ahold of a pretty red bitch like me. I was too fragile, and my expiration date was not about to kick in for at least another sixty years.

Quickly closing the door back, I pulled out my phone and dialed Melly's number. The rings were slow and dragging for what felt like forever.

By the time I heard his voice come through the receiver, my Kaycake side had come out.

"Hello?"

"Melly! Baby, somebody is posted outside my job asking about me. They got guns. They know you, but I don't think I wanna know them," I whined like the huge child I was.

"What? Who's outside your job? Are you okay?" he asked me seriously. I could hear the calmness slide right out of him.

"Uhh, they work for the Johnny Cochran's firm, and they're trying to win us a lawsuit for the damn establishment I'm about to die in, Melly. Of course, I don't know who they are. All I understood was the gun in his hand and the name Kay-Kay," I stressed nearly in tears.

"Are you able to hide? I'm on the way. Are they near you?"

I could hear him shuffling through some things and climb inside of his car while he spoke to me.

Taking a look outside the clinic room's door, I didn't see anyone trying to break in, so that was enough certainty for me.

"We're in the back of the dentist's office. The doors are locked. Please hurry, Melly. I'm scared."

I ended the call knowing that he was about to crash the entire city to get near me, but the police were damn sure about being contacted for extra backup in case the killers wanted to go out with a bang. I didn't need Melly getting in any trouble, so arriving with a gun would probably end up in a bad spot for him. Following my instincts, I tossed the phone to my co-worker.

"Here, girl. Call 911 and tell them what's going on!"

The crazy-ass hoe stared at me for a second too long but still placed them three digits on that dial. Now all I could do was just sit back and hope that our help arrives before Thing number 1 and 2 came crashing through the front of those glass doors.

* * *

Melly

Looking down at my watch, the time was 7:30 P.M., and I was mashing the pedal down Cascade to reach the Small Smiles Center where Kay-Kay worked. The only thing running through my mind was making sure my queen didn't get hurt behind some shit me, or Bleeko was involved in. That shit right there would force me to lose it. I had no intentions of sparing whoever was outside of this building, and I doubted highly if they felt any different. By the time I was speeding past the Allen Temple apartment complex. I spotted the hue of police lights glistening in the air. The plaza parking space was filled with cruisers, and sure enough, they were all posted in front of the dentistry.

Jolting my car across the street, I turned recklessly into the drive-thru and jumped out when I spotted Kay-Kay sitting in the back of a police cruiser with tears flushing down her face. Rushing over to the car, a duty officer stopped me with a hand on the shoulder.

"Hey, buddy. No one is allowed through here at the moment."

"Man, that's my wife. Get the fuck off me." I smacked his arm forcefully.

He moved to grab me until a leading official stepped in between us. It was the same black man from earlier. Detective Solomon was what his badge said.

"What's the problem here? Didn't I have a run-in with you this afternoon already? I thought I said to stay off the radar, Hicks?" His nose was flaring up with anger as he reached for his cuffs.

"Fuck all that. My girl is in the back of that cruiser. Someone was trying to hurt her. Now I haven't done shit motherfucker, so get my girl to me immediately, or you'll have a reason to kill me out here tonight, sir!" I stated with my muscles tensed in case they tried to restrain me.

Solomon glared at me but still waved towards one of his rookies to let my baby out of that backseat. When I saw her run towards me in tears, it crumbled my heart. I know she was scary as hell, so anything dealing with a gun surely had her shook. Pulling her into my arms, I kissed her cheek, whispering into her ear. "Calm down; I'm here. I'm here."

"Mr. Hicks, I'm not sure what occurred here tonight, but you might want to be glad we got here before these dudes got out of hand and fled. Do you know if anyone has a reason to try and hurt you guys for any reason?"

"Nah, unfortunately, this is the type of shit that goes on in your area, remember. If there is nothing left for my girl to handle with you people, I would like to take her home, please."

Officer Solomon acted like he wanted to make a slick comment, and his sergeant still mugged as if he had a problem from me pushing his ass off me. Instead of giving me more of a hard time. He nodded. "Continue on, Hicks."

Moving Kay-Kay through the crowded area, we made it to the car. I helped her into the passenger seat and climbed back behind the wheel. I made my way out of the plaza, heading for our home. My mind was now on the fuckery, and I was about to address it firsthand. Tonight.

Chapter 12
Melly

After dropping Kay-Kay off, I made my way down to Silent Avenue in search of this nigga Bleeko. I couldn't say that I didn't see this shit coming because I've always seen the signs but never knew that it would actually come to me beefing with the same nigga that I came up with. The entire hood heard about the shit Bleeko pulled in the store a few weeks back, not including the life of the little girl that was taken away for some extra shit he had going on. I decided to cut ties and allow him to move on his own, but when it came down to him jeopardizing my family for his mistakes, it was going to end horribly for him, and I was gonna be the one to prove that.

After sitting in the cut behind Sanabella's with my lights off for about twenty minutes, I spotted Bleeko's Lexus pull in front of the Tasty Dog restaurant. He hopped out of his car, flashing his fake ass grill like shit was all good. I knew for a fact that he had love on the block, enough love to make a turn against me. I was never the type to be crossed, and that trait was after my father birthed me.

Grabbing my pistol from the middle console, I tucked it in my pants and got out. My figure blended in with the darkness allowing me to push up the cut with the quickness. With my .45 automatic pistol in hand, I timed that shit perfectly. Right before he could slide over to the section where his little saviors, Trev and Dunk stood, I slid from around the building, sticking my gun in the center of his face.

"You got some nerve, fuck nigga!" I spat with malice.

Bleeko's face glowed like a deer in the headlights, and the movement on the block instantly stopped once all eyes landed on us. His face was balled up like he couldn't believe that I was the one standing in front of him, prepared to take his life for playing Ford tough like he wasn't pussy without a crew.

"Melly," he chuckled, looking down at the concrete. "Have you hit a rock or somethin', nigga? Cause if not, I would advise you to get that strap out of my face before I start to feel like you really trying to hurt me."

I already knew in my mind that it was me against mostly every individual that posted around at the moment. Trev and Dunk removed their guns, forcing me to rack my handgun back to make them clowns think before they tried anything ridiculous. This shit was personal, and that's exactly how I planned on handling it. One on one.

"You lied to me. You mixed my name in that shit, and that's not Silent Avenue. I had nothing to do with that."

Bleeko's smile forced me to grow angry quicker than quick. Slapping him in the mouth with the gun, I watched him hit the ground before Trev and Dunk could react. Bleeko raised a hand, standing back to his feet. "Hold up, hold up. Don't shoot him. He's like a nephew to me."

"Fuck that shit you talkin! You go, we go nigga. Let us bust this nigga, Bleek," Trev snarled, feeling like he was ready to take me on. Little did he know my mind was willing to risk it all tonight, especially when it came down to the love of my life.

Bleeko still denied his request, motioning him to lower the gun. "Nah, we don't kill family. We handle it like men. I'll shoot him a fair one and excuse this mistake." He looked at me as if we were on the same page.

The block stood around, now motionless, wondering what was next to occur between me and this nigga. It was a point in time where I felt like Bleeko was the brother I never had, but at that moment, while I stared deep into his eyes and into his soul, I could see the enemy that had been betraying me for the longest.

Dunk moved closer to us, and I was sure to keep my eyes focused on him in case he played crazy. I was surprised when he stepped a few feet away from us, humbly speaking.

"Melly, I'm not hip to what the fuck y'all two got going on, but the one thing I can't allow y'all to do is murder each other. I'm not picking sides, and if it can't be handled the real Silent way, then one of y'all need to walk off and never return. Ya feel me?" he questioned, showing the two guns that were attached to his waist.

I wanted to shoot his ass first and make a full roundhouse with Bleeko and the block, but so many people were posted with their eyes glued. If I let off a shot, there was no telling if I would make it home without being hit with every gun a nigga was toting at that moment.

"Put the gun down, Melly," Dunk asked me with a calm tone.

I stared deep into Bleeko's eyes while weighing the options in my head. Spotting Cat step through the crowd to reach me, he nodded his head, giving me the confirmation to listen. I exhaled before placing the gun in his hand and didn't hesitate to deliver a solid punch to his right jaw.

Once the first swing was initiated, Bleeko shook off the blow and squared up with me like a real gangsta.

"It's not gonna go the way you think, baby boy," he spat with hatred as we circled around each other.

I tried my best to beat the blood out of his ass while the block held out their phones, recording us like two animals out of the city zoo. Every time I struck his ass, he was splitting like a bruised banana. The punches he gave back were a good effort, but not enough to place a whole fool like me out for the count.

After chunking our fist for the next five minutes, I sent Bleeko crashing to the ground with a right hook. Even though I was tired, I still could see that he didn't have an ounce of fight left in his body. Before I could climb on top to put his ass to sleep, Dunk put a hand on my chest.

"Melly, that's enough, my nigga. Nothing else to prove, lil bro. Whatever he did, I'm sure he understands now. It's over."

I was out of breath, and my head was thumping like a rock against the side of the garage. Grabbing my gun from Cat's hand, I walked back over to my car, jumping behind the wheel to swerve off. A part of my heart said that I could have handled shit a lot better, but my intuitions told me to follow my first mind. Bleeko was a snake, one that couldn't be trusted. I failed with letting him play under me, but I damn sure learned a valuable lesson. Dog would always eat dog.

As I turned to pull out of the parking lot, my vision spotted a familiar woman standing on the curb watching me through my car window like a hawk. Her face didn't show anger, neither did she look to possess any hostility as she grilled me down. I didn't recognize until I drove past her that it was little Denaisha's mother. The murdered child that was involved with the reckless shootout a few days back. I could feel a lump form in my throat as she continued to eye my car. Not because of nervousness, but from the look of disappointment, she carried in her pupils. Something told me to go back and place a bullet into Bleeko's head, regardless of the consequences. I just truly knew that it still wouldn't change what was at hand. Silent Avenue didn't feel like home anymore, and that only meant one thing. The hood was on the verge of crossing me out of the game. They just didn't know that I kept my own set of rules in the tuck.

Chapter 13
Bleeko

I couldn't stop looking at my face in the mirror as I sipped the patron straight out of the bottle. I had to snort a line of white girl just to subside the pain, and the thought of how Melly tried to shine on the block was eating at me like a junkie needing a fix. After punching the fifth hole in my living room wall, I was finally done with even feeling sorry for the young idiot. There was so much he didn't know, hit that could have him in a casket within the next few days. Things that would make his miserable little life crumble to pieces.

My phone vibrating on the glass table forced me to look down. Once I viewed the name, a small sense of doubt climbed into my mind. It wasn't the feeling of me failing to handle my business, but the doubt of this idiot that sat in the big chair crossing me out on a promise that meant everything to me, regardless of what Melly and I had transgressing against each other at the time.

Picking it up, I prepared myself to go ahead and get the dragging-ass news out the way, so I can continue with my business that was at hand.

"You ducking my call or somethin', nigga? I've been calling."

I didn't know what the hell this nigga had on his mental, but being the head honcho of this little operation didn't mean shit to me. My respect was still gonna be given, with or without him.

"Man, listen, Sal. I can hear more than well, so you can calm down with all the screaming inside a nigga's eardrum, bruh!"

"Nah, fool. You're four phone calls late, and to be honest, I'm not thinking that you care about the severity of this matter.

125

Did you find it?" he asked with his raspy, dry voice straining through the line.

I knew I couldn't even argue with this clown, but I knew that my problems would at least be in the clear after handling the present affairs with Big Sal. Still, I had to keep shit funky.

"Nah, I haven't, but I know he has it," I assured him while looking at my swollen face for the hundredth time.

I could hear a slight sound of agitation release from his lips, a little too quiet to figure his expression.

"If what you saying was true, why don't you have it?"

"Because I don't know where he sleeps yet. I'm not a fucking spy. I can't use x-ray vision to find the shit Sal," I tried to use common sense to him before I grew mad.

"Love. That's what you wanted to show this guy. You're so weak that you're forgetting the entire mission. Too much compassion throws the mercy out of the window when you're too weak. I could have just had Joe Boy find this fool and end it all."

The comment sparked a sense of madness on my mental, but I would never let him see me sweat. If anything, he was playing himself right into a trap, and I was about to allow it.

"Maybe that's a good idea because I'm not doing the dirty work anymore. I'm through with this shit, and now, you, Joe Boy, and whoever else is behind this bullshit can move whatever piece you want on the chessboard, but it won't be me," I snapped, hanging up the line in his face.

The pity I had on Melly for so long was now about to go down the drain, and it wasn't gonna end well. A pretty price was on his head. A ticket he would never be able to accommodate unless he replaced his life with the payday. My position of being around him for so many years held the demons away. Now that we were on different sides of the street, it was time for the games to begin.

Nightmare on Silent Avenue

* * *

Kay-Kay

I was so nervous at the moment; I didn't know what to do. It had been almost four hours since Melly dropped me off at home, and I still had yet to know that he was okay. My mind was running so fast that I had to turn on the news to ensure my baby hadn't been abducted by some niggas and chopped up in the Chattahoochee River. The main topic was still about the precious baby Denaisha losing her life a few days back. A clip of her mother expressing her pain was going viral, and upon seeing it, I stopped to hear the words of what she wanted to see occur come from her mouth.

"My baby was gunned down in the bounds of this city. She was taken away from me before she could even walk across the stage for elementary graduation. I want this criminal brought to justice, quick and immediate. Please. For my daughter, Denaisha," she spoke with grief while the flashing cameras caught every tear that dribbled down her cheeks. I felt her pain, but it also gave me butterflies knowing that Melly was possibly one of those men that were involved with that baby being slain like a known drug dealer in the neighborhood.

Picking up my cell, I was about to try calling again until I heard a set of keys being used to open my front door.

Jumping up from the couch, I faced Melly just as he stepped through our threshold. His face was slightly bruised, and I could tell from specs of blood on his shirt that something didn't go too well, wherever he was showing back up from. Walking over to him, I kissed his lips, pulling him into my arms just for a moment of comfort. "Are you okay, Melly? Please tell me you didn't do nothing crazy?" I asked, looking up into his eyes.

Watching him lock the door and sit on the couch, he ignored my question as if I wasn't even visible at the moment.

"Melly, I'm talking to you."

"You act like I can't hear you, Kay-Kay. I'm not really in the mood for conversation, baby. Just fall back."

I couldn't believe the way he was talking to me, even after sitting up, waiting for him to arrive home safe. The past few days had his attitude rising as he spent more time in the streets.

"Well, excuse me for worrying, Melly. You walk out of the house and come back with blood all over you as if I would just smile and ask did you have a great time on your little murder spree. What has gotten into you?" I stood in front of him, trying my best to conceal the way he was making me feel.

"I handled my business, Kay. There's nothing else to ask." He stood up, heading for the bedroom.

I could see that his mind was definitely elsewhere, and I wasn't respecting the way his ass was disrespecting with the negative energy he carried back into our home with him.

"Oh, nothing else to say, huh? I guess it'll be mutual if I leave and stay over at my parents' until you get your mind together. Would it be anything to say about that?"

"Maybe it is. I don't give a damn. You pick. I'm sitting here risking my life for what? For you to be a spoiled ass brat while I got niggas gunning at me!"

His slanted lashes and red eyes looked like he had gone mad. He was raising his arm like he was gonna hit me, and I could see it as we stood off, waiting for the other to back down. I could feel the seal of my eyelids watering, and before I knew it, tears drenched my cheekbones.

"So, I guess you feel the same way about our marriage? What about the visions I've been seeing? You never tried to see it my way, Melly. I guess you have to keep it Silent Avenue, right? What about when prison comes knocking? Who's gotta suffer then? Because we both know it's not you." I pointed a finger to his nose.

I was heated, and he really was on the verge of making me saying sit to the motherfucking left. Just when I thought he might soften up, he crushed my heart with his next foolish ass statement.

"You'll either cut your non-sense, or I'll just head to my cousin's spot on Silent Avenue. You can have all this right here to ya self. Just say it."

Without question, I turned my back regardless of how bad it killed me not to. This was the man that I loved, acting like he was just fed up with all that we've worked so hard to build. He was truly the king that I felt would rescue me from the hell bounds of single life, but I guess things were really changing.

Slamming the front door behind me, I hopped into my BMW and backed out of the driveway with a hurt spirit and a foolish mind. Melly was pushing the crash out button, and I saw it coming a mile away. Maybe space is what he needed. It was my true hope to keep our love consistent and not separate cause he was damn sho' slanging. It was really my man. He was my meat disposal when I chose, and I was gonna stand up for what was mines sho' nuff.

I knew just the person to help, I was thinking before I pulled out my Pixel phone and made that call. Of course, it was always an answer on the first ring.

"Kayona? What is it, baby? It's almost 12:00," My mother's voice soothed me instantly.

"I need you, ma. I'm on my way over," I spoke with defeat.

"Kayona, you're scaring me, girl. Tell me what's wrong. I can only take so much now," she begged.

"Me and Melly had a fight. I think he wants to break up," I confessed with a slight sob.

"Get here now, and I'll be up waiting for you. Do you hear me?"

"Yes, ma'am."

The one thing I could say bout Mrs. Wilcox, my mama, she was my knight in shining armor before I knew what love was. I needed her to get through this phase.

Chapter 13
Melly
Martin Luther King Dr.

Highway 626 was the exit which was awkward cause I never felt the devil actually ride my back as if I were paralyzed for hours, forced me to get on the road and seek attention. The sky was blurry with clouds. I nearly ran off the road a few minutes earlier. The image of the old dead woman appeared in the middle of the road, forcing me to jump the sidewalk. By the time I guided my car back on track, I had noticed that I was on my old childhood street. Eason Street. Do you know what was even more surreal? For some strange reason, that scenery looked so familiar. Once I noticed that I was now staring out the passenger window. Tupac's song, *Hail Mary,* started to beat through the speakers. Jerking my head to the side of me, I stared at the caramel complexion man, bobbing his head and ignoring me like he didn't have a care in the world. A silver bracelet was on his wrist, glistening like a new day. His long body frame was wrapped in a Coogi sweater and a pair of Versace slacks. He resembled my dad so much.

As we got closer to my old home, I rotated my eyes back to the window l could see a man stepping out on the porch.

The Tupac track was still beating. "Come with me. Hail Mary… What do we have here now? Do ya wanna ride or die? La'da, da, da, da, da, da."

As we grew closer, I watched as the man raised his hand, pointing towards us. Something was in his hand. I was squinting to try and detect what it may have been.

"There go ya Uncle Franklin, son. Do you wanna stop?" the man next to me asked.

Before I could reply to his complicating question, the sound of gunshots began to erupt. I could feel the first bullet strike me in the jaw. The burning sensation started to surface through my body as I tried to duck from the slugs rushing through the glass windows. I could hear the painful grunts escape the man's lips next to me, confirming that he was getting the bad end of what was occurring. As the wreckage came to a halt, I laid against the man's shoulder as he slumped into the driver's seat. Tupac's voice was the last thing I remember before the darkness started to fade across the back of my eyelids. The smell of thick fire rose through my nostrils, and my breathing ceased.

Jumping out of my sleep, I looked around for Kay-Kay. The thought of our fight crossed my brain wave, and I instantly remembered the regret I felt from the argument that took place earlier that night. The clock read 6:01 A.M, and a cool chill was running down my spine. I felt death approaching me, and for some reason, I knew that I wouldn't make it out if I didn't try to change. Nothing could keep me on this earth but God and the deeds of my own hands. I knew I was ready.

* * *

M.L.K. DRIVE
Citgo Gas Station
8:43 A.M.

Even though the sun was shining bright, and people were moving about happily, I still wasn't joyous at all. My energy felt so bad at the moment, and for some reason, I couldn't stop thinking about Kay-Kay. I attempted to call her phone at least thirty times and still got no answer. I was distraught as a motherfucker. I really didn't care about shit, but getting my baby back and straightening the hell up so that I could be the man she knew I was. All that was running across my track at the time was unbelievable, but it was about to change, and it was gonna start with me. After calling back up the Muslim brother Muhammad this morning, He agreed to meet up and give me the lessons on how to pray and embrace Islam. True enough, it may not have an effect on me right away, but showing some sort of fear to God was better than living like I was superior.

Pulling a small turn into the gas station, I parked directly in front of the store and spotted Muhammad coming out of the entrance. He carried two small cups of coffee and a couple of blueberry muffins in his hands. Of course, his Quran was tucked under his armpit. Leaning across the seat, I opened the door allowing him access to slide inside.

"Assalamu alaikum, young brother. I got us some here to snack on while we make this drive. I was surprised when you called, but it's alhamdulillah that you're ready to join with this religion for the greater good." He passed me a cup of coffee before closing the door.

"Yeah, man. I think it's time, ya know. Kind of getting into it with my girl and having some personal issues. Just too much going on. I'm not really into the drag session, so I'll be straightforward. Do you really feel like this will help me?"

"I think that's something you have to gauge for yourself, Meltavious. Allah has worked a miracle for me to change my life, and he can possibly do the same for you if it's truly what you desire. Let's take a ride. I wanna show you something."

His energy was high enough to influence me that he was right, and I couldn't waste any more time wondering what if. It was time to let Silent Avenue go and start clean.

As I placed the car in reverse and dispersed from the parking lot, I found myself driving, locked into a deep conversation about what was ahead of me with Muhammad. It was crazy how I felt at peace, explaining my problems to this complete stranger. He wasn't the type to speak too fast or give a harsh reply to something that wasn't understood. It felt like all could be great if I could follow his path, but I didn't see the dark rocky road that came along with walking down that journey.

I found myself pulling down Silent Avenue in the mix of heading in Muhammad's direction and made a quick stop. As soon as my car came to a halt, I spotted Cat coming through the cut. He took a few steps towards my car when he saw it, but froze for some apparent reason. He started to shake his head, waving a hand in front of his neck like it wasn't safe to get out of the car or something. Watching him turn around, he broke off running with two of them damn cats trailing behind. It was probably another phase, and that's a stage nobody liked to see Cat go through.

Throwing it quickly out of my head, I looked over to the brother Muhammad. "Is there anything you need out of the store?"

I noticed that his face was balled up, but he declined my offer. After running into the corner shop to handle my quick business, I ran back out and hopped into the driver's seat and swerved back into traffic.

"So, where we headed to?" I asked, trying to see what he had, so magnificent to show me.

Cracking a light smile, he pointed to the next left that was coming up by Burbank and Troy Street.

"A place that always soothes my spirit. I'm taking you to someone that actually helped me find guidance."

Chapter 14
Bleeko

Bumping my stereo to the max, I pulled the new Benz truck that I just copped a couple of weeks ago out of the garage. It was a fresh day to grind, and my small stumbles damn sho' wasn't about to stop me from winning like a true boss should. Now that my hands were free of Melly and his new troubles, all I had to do was get the cheddar and make it look good for the city. I didn't need everybody looking at me with a pointed finger in case his ass came up with a slug to the back of his noggin.

Spotting Nina in the American Legion Club's parking lot, I turned in to see if she was willing to cough up a little tongue fun for my day to start of sweeter than a bag of Jolly Ranchers. As my whip came to a stop beside her, she looked down into my eyes, and I could see that she wasn't the usual Nina that was on Silent Avenue ready to pop her shit daily. She looked more frightened to see me personally. I could sense it.

"What's wrong?" I asked, looking at her with a suspicious eye.

Her head lowered to the ground, alerting me that shit wasn't right. "Bleek, they found Latoya dead behind the elementary school on Ashby."

"What the fuck that gotta do with me?" I checked her ass immediately.

"You didn't have to do her like that, Bleeko." She backed away from my car with her hands up in the air like I was trying to hurt her or some shit.

Before I could even snap or think about my next action, the wailing of police sirens started to blare through my ears, and I could see the swarm of cruisers blocking off every exit through my rearview. Slamming the whip into reverse, I tried to back out and was rear-ended by an unmarked Crown Victoria. Two officers protruded from the car with their guns drawn. The rest of the force followed suit and aimed straight for my vehicle in case I got any bright ideas for fleeing. Realizing I was blocked in completely, I raised my hands up to be sure I wasn't shot, and once my car door came flinging open. Detective Solomon was snatching me out. Tossing me on the ground, he placed a knee into my back.

"Brandon June. It's been a long run for you, bro, but I'm afraid it has to come to an end. Search the car." He pointed a finger at his cadets to move.

His eyes were piercing down on me with disgust, but it was nothing I had to worry about if shit happened to go sour. My road was not heading to prison, and I would do whatever to prove that shit. My mind instantly thought about the ounce of dope that was in my glove compartment. Just as I said that, one of them was holding that shit out of the window like they had hounds with them searching.

"You know I can't save you this time, right idiot? The Hunter Hills and the Denaisha case is pointing towards you, Brandon. You've drowned ya self, fool. They've got witnesses," he was whispering in my ear like my journey for life was over.

"I'm clean, Solomon. You know that. I wouldn't lie to you. I ain't have nothin' to do with that," I lied, feeling like he was bluffing. They all knew I was the hood dealer, and this was a scheme to take me down. My name and reputation would stand behind me for sho.

"Oh yeah? Ms. Latoya Ritter says that she's willing to testify on you if we keep you in the slammer forever, stupid. You put heat on yourself, and I have to still follow the law."

I couldn't believe the words that were escaping out of his mouth. He was really about to lock me the fuck up. "Ain't no way you're serious right now. You gotta be busting juices out my balls, Solomon June. You're my brother still, or you must have forgotten after you moved off and left us," I seethed in a low tone where the protruding officers didn't hear.

This nigga leaned dead in my face and laughed. "They already know that dumb-dumb. You just established that a few seconds ago. You better hope you can get a fucking bond, retard. My days for pulling strings for you aren't the same anymore, Brandon. I'm a damn police officer, for crying out loud. I didn't leave anybody. I was forced away, and you know that," he matched my attitude back with a little more aggression.

"You have the right to remain silent. Anything you say can and will be used on you in the court of law. You have the right to an attorney. If you can't afford one, it will be appointed. You're under arrest for the murder of Denaisha Spencer and Lonnie Wimbush of the Hunter Hills Super Market," he stated, placing me in cuffs.

"This is bullshit. You think you can just do this. I'm innocent nigga. We family. You gotta believe me, Solomon!" I stressed.

My heart dropped once I spotted one of the cops interrupt us with the two guns that were used in my shootout the other night. Forgetting to ditch them, I tossed them into a bag under my spare tire for a few days and forgot all about them. My head dropped when he raised them both up by the handle.

"Well, I guess we gotta case after all. Please take Mr. June in for booking at Fulton County Jail. He'll be seeing a judge," Solomon ordered, bagging the evidence with a straight face.

I looked on sadly as the officers drug me over to a cruiser, throwing me in the back and pulling off. I knew for a fact that if my prints showed up on that weapon, I could call it quits for ever seeing the free world again. Just as my mind pondered on my next move, Melly popped through my brain. It was either him or me, and Bleeko always won.

Chapter 15
Kay-Kay
Eight and a Half Hours Later
Her Parents Home, Buckhead

The smell of burning flesh was hitting me heavy as I watched the torturing flames coming from underneath the door. Backing up, I ran for the bathroom and slammed the door behind me. I pressed my hands against the wood, and my eyes glared up at the sticky sign that boasted the number 626. I turned around, and the sight of Melly bounded to a chair appeared in front of me. One gunshot was fresh to the side of his head, and the image of the bloody old woman was standing behind his. It was as if she owned him, his soul. I couldn't scream, neither could I move my legs. Her dead black eyes pleaded for me to feel her pain. The more she twitched and moved towards me, and my heart decreased to another pace. The next thing I knew, Melly's dead body spoke in a wretched and horrific tone.

"Wake up, Kay-Kay. Save me, Queen. Wake up! The nightmare is over!"

Snapping out of the devastating dream, I sat up with the quickness, dropping the throwaway phone Melly swapped out a few a day's back. The battery was on the floor, sitting on top of a piece of notebook paper, and the phone was flipped over by the second sofa piece. Picking up the battery first, I scooped up the paper and scanned it quickly.

"Please text me asap. Jemora. #4043338989 I have to talk to you."

The shit instantly caused me to get hot, and the nerve of him trying to hide a woman's number in the back of his cell was even more deceiving. I definitely couldn't take the news if I really found out that he was moving on with another one. My mind said to dial the bitch's number and ask every question while demanding every answer. Luckily, I always played the game raw when it came to being ahead of the game. After calling his spare line and getting the voicemail three times, I turned on the find me app that I programmed to his phone the same night he bought it. I refused to let his ass think Kayona Wilcox was losing out on my family and future because his ass was gonna have a death date before that occurred. The dream I just had scared me drastically, and a bad feeling was creeping over my head. Watching the app upload and locate Melly's phone location, the address maximized to my screen. My eyes grew wide in disbelief, but I was damn sure not catching z's when I read out the address.

"626 Scott Lane."

It was never a place I was aware of him hanging before, and the weird-ass number 626 was asking to be seen. It wasn't a coincidence, and I'll be damn what a heffa could tell me. I was experiencing some real Ms. Cleo shit, and my mind was telling me to get to Melly.

Watching my mother and father step through the front door, they paused, noticing my troubled face. My father was the first to speak.

"Kay. What's up, baby girl?"

"Are you okay, honey? I know you're probably still going through a bit of emotion. We're here for you, pudding," my mama added, giving me a look of empathy.

"I need you two to take me somewhere. I think Melly's in trouble. I'm worried, and he's not picking up his phone." I chewed on my nails in a panic. If Melly was really hurt, that meant no life was gonna make it through my bones because he gave me all the soul and life that I carried within me. I know rushing back to him may seem crazy for a parent, but for a woman who cherished a man, I truly felt was worth more to me, whether they chose to agree or not."

"What do you mean trouble? Is he okay? He hasn't gotten hurt, has he?" Mr. Benjamin questioned with a turned-up nose.

"I'm not sure, dad. All I know is I have to make sure I don't lose him. He's all I got. Regardless of trials, family don't turn their back. He still a part of us," I poured out my feelings to my father, ready to cry if he denied me to ensure the love of my life was still in his right senses.

"Benjamin, we have to help him. Whatever it is, do it please," my mama helped tag team with her pouty face and dramatic tone.

Watching my dad huff. He folded his arms. "What is it you need me to do, Kayona?"

"Take me to an address. I need to see him."

"And what if he's with the same problems, Kay? What if he is a guy that doesn't care whether you live a great life or not? It's not your job to chase him if he confesses to loving you. Don't you understand that, sweetheart?" he tried to explain with his fatherly opinion, and truly I didn't want to hear that.

"Dad, I'm asking you to help me keep my happiness. This is what I want. And this is what I will have. I believe in what I have, and who are you to tell me I'm wrong? Melly gave me hope when I didn't think I could make it on love before. He never showed me a side to say that he didn't care for me wholeheartedly. And if my forgiveness could stretch out for him, I felt that you guys could do the same."

Both of my parents gazed at each other before taking a moment to think.

My dad was the first to nod in disappointment, but his words showed me that I still held the soft spot in his chest.

"Listen, baby girl. I know you love this guy, but me losing you or watching suffering overtake you isn't worth any man or amount of money on this earth. I cherish you and your

141

mother because I know it was my duty to provide and do right by you two, as any man should. So, your pain is mine. I can promise you that if this turns out badly with the way I pictured, it won't end too good. Now let's go and get my son-in-law." He cracked a smile, holding out his arms.

Rushing over to hug his neck, I squeezed him tightly. We all trailed out of the house on a mission to correct the wrongs for the sake of our family. I just didn't know that it would nearly cost so much.

Chapter 16
Melly

After arriving at Muhammad's destination on the South Side of Atlanta, I parked my car in front of the one-level beige-colored home.

"We're here. Come on in. Let me show you around," he offered, stepping out of the car.

Climbing out of my front seat, I walked into the yard with him and raised my head when a woman stepped out of the front door. A young boy was in her arms, and she looked the exact same way she did the last time they were able to have contact. She sported an all-white $N^0 21$ skirt with a Jill Stuart halter top. Her hair was laid neatly down her back, and a light coat of makeup was on her face, giving her skin a beautiful glow. She paused like seeing a ghost after finally noticing me coming into the yard. It was the chick from the barbershop. Once again, her face said that I was some bullshit for never calling. And judging from the way she was locked in on me, I think she wanted to chump me at the time.

Her posture straightened when walking past Muhammad, and she tried her best not to make eye contact with me. That gave the cue that nothing was supposed to be said.

"Where are you going?" He stopped with a stern expression.

"Me and Kemon are going out for a walk around Centennial Park. We're just wanna get out for a while. That's all. I'm not taking him around anybody." She swallowed her spit, nodding repeatedly.

Muhammad stared for a slight second too long, and I could feel the tension between them wasn't right.

"Okay. Be back on time. Keep your distance from people. Wouldn't need you getting distracted."

"Sure thing."

Even though she replied with a smile, I sensed her fear. She didn't even look him in the eyes as he chastised her like a child. As she continued to her parked Ford Expedition, I watched her turn back at me, shaking her head with a sorrowful face.

I kept my eye trained on her until Muhammad and I walked through the side garage door. Deactivating his alarm, he waved for me to follow him.

I allowed him to lead the way and slowed down immediately when my pupils landed on the parked 2004 Candy apple red Cadillac. Slowly walking past it, I scanned the license plate that read "2 Fresh". The same silver trimming was aligned around the rims and fender, and the flashback of my dreams crossed my mind once I placed a finger on the hood.

"Whose car is this?" I asked with a curious worry.

Muhammad turned back to look and smiled. "That old thing? It's my brother, Kato's. He died about twenty years back. I've had it since but don't really take it for a spin much often. Maybe one day I can show ya how she rides." He smirked with joy.

"Yeah, maybe," I agreed as we continued inside his home.

The bounds of his kitchen and living room were magnificent with the decor and vibe. There was such a chill vibe to his domain, and the quiet energy made it feel like the most comfortable home in the world. Most of his furniture was from Paris. Expensive glass sculptures of animals were posted around the entire den, and I saw one big cashmere rug spread across the living room floor as we entered the large family area.

"Make yourself at home, Meltavious. I'll get you a soda, and a new Quran, my brother. Please sit down." He motioned towards the comfortable-looking couch.

Once he disappeared, my mind switched over to the decision I was about to make. I was really about to take my faith to the religion of Islam, and I was nervous. Not just for me changing, but for my wife and family actually seeing it for themselves.

Standing up, I walked over to the table, glancing at all the framed pictures. Some were photos of Muslim men offering prayer, a few people that were probably related to him, and another one that grabbed my attention. It was a shot of eight young boys standing next to each other, maybe an old school picture. One of the guys looked familiar, but you could clearly see they were all picked on in school.

The feeling that someone was watching me came across my flesh like the devil sniffing the fear out of a small child. The hairs on my arm and neck stood up. When I turned around, I exhaled, realizing I was still alone.

The time on my watch said 7:43, and I needed to finish my process in order to try and reach Kaycake about making my change. I knew it would brighten her spirit and my own. As I thought about how great things would be from this day on out, I spotted a large picture of a woman mounted over the front door. Squinting my eyes to get a better view, Muhammad eased back into the section of the home.

"You like the aura, huh?" he asked.

"Yeah, it kind of feels like home. Who is that?" I pointed to the familiar woman resting over the home's entrance.

Muhammad chuckled but still answered. "Man, that's the queen of it all. The woman who gave up everything to see her bloodline win. That's Mama June."

The name rang through my ears loud and clear. As I kept staring at the lady's photo, I recognized that she was the woman from my dreams. My heartbeat thumped heavily, and I could feel the air leave me as I pictured the blood rushing down her face like in my sleep. As I turned to face Muhammad, I felt a hard thump crash across my head.

As shit started to go black, I called his name right before falling to the carpet and blacking out. It took me a minute to shake off the dizziness once I woke up and got myself together. I had been sitting in the same spot for the past forty minutes, so my body felt numb. Coming back to reality, Muhammad stepped in front of me with a loaded handgun. His face wasn't warm anymore, and he roughly checked all my pockets as another voice started to speak.

"Make sure he's able to function. I need to be sure he understands the severity of what's at stake."

The tone was raspy and unfamiliar, but it wasn't too many people that had the guts to try me and be successful with whatever they had in mind.

"Muhammad, what's going on?" I was breathing erratically, thinking that changing my ways was supposed to be the main topic, but after seeing the gun in his hand, I knew that was out of the story.

"I can tell you that young gun," the voice sounded off again. This time a wheelchair came rolling from the dark hallway, and the sight of a young dude appeared in front of me. He was holding a double-barrel shotgun, and half of his face was disfigured from what appeared to be a war wound. His skin was rough, and a death-like gaze was spilling from his sockets. He snickered for a few seconds and greeted me.

"Good ass day, ain't it, Melly? I thought you would come to visit soon enough," he addressed like I knew who the fuck his creepy ass was.

Spitting out a ball of blood mixed with saliva caught my breath, then spoke.

"I'm not sure if you have the wrong Melly, but I don't know you, my guy. Maybe you have me confused."

He laughed loudly, holding the bridge of his nose like I said something so dumb. Muhammad was still quiet, standing behind me where I had to glance in the mirror that sat directly across to see his face.

"How about I tell you a story, Melly. One that you actually might like, being that you play a major part in it. This is gonna be a small biography of eight young boys that had their entire life ahead of them. That is until one started to get too many passes on things that a few of us others felt entitled to. My mama, June, was the sweetest woman in the world. When she wasn't assisting the school hall with tutoring, she was helping the orphanage that was out on the Northside. I used to like the job she had; I mean, that was until she decided to come home with four new boys who we didn't know shit about. One of those guys was your loveable dad, Franklin."

My ears opened like a dark portal hearing my father's name. I knew for a fact I didn't know the grim reaper-looking motherfucker in front of me, but saying the name Franklin had me wondering who the hell I was really in the same room with.

"Yeah, that's right nigga. Yo' dad. It was four of them adopted and moved into my house, where my grandma already had enough on her hands. My dad, Kato, was man enough to take care of the family, but the day she allowed those four rejects to enter our house, she committed suicide. See, Franklin was like the best in Mama June's eyes. Like literally this pussy nigga could do no wrong to her. Not only did he take my dad's spot, but he took his heart and mines too. See, Granny ended up striking gold for some real loot. Instead of her allowing the blessing to be spread through us all, she decided to let Franklin think of a way to hold this money until it was the right time to give it to us. And it's taken me twenty years to find out how slick that bitch was."

"You don't know shit about my dad or me. I'm not sure what you two got in mind with me, but it'll all end badly before I go out alone," I threatened, feeling a bad scenario playing out in my head.

Rolling the wheelchair slightly closer, where I could see all his wounds clearly, he sucked his teeth and continued. "Your dad and my father had words about this money, and at the time, I was too young to understand what family tribulations were. The only day I remember is the one where Franklin gunned him and me down like we didn't share the same last name. All over a misunderstanding. I remember the bullets that hit me, the Tupac song that was beating while my dad died in front of me." He stared at me with hatred.

"Those are lies. I don't believe you. My dad had no reason to cross anyone out, especially a bunch of non- relatives," I shot back with anger.

A strong punch from Muhammad's right hand caused me to bite my lip, sending blood all over the white carpet. "Don't speak like that Meltavious, Show some respect."

I didn't like the wheel punch, but I couldn't do anything, but roll with the way shit was playing at the moment and pray that God found me a way out because I was still confused and needed the first escape route that I could find.

"Melly, your dad hid nine million dollars of cash from us that Mama June hit the number for. I got so tired of her speaking about this nigga that once I found out she struck for the money, I had my uncle here to go and take care of her old ass too. It was the easiest way to kill two birds at once. Regardless of how things ended with my father and uncles, Franklin still has something that belongs to me, and I want it. Where's the bracelet, Melly?"

My mind was lost for words, and the thought of my dad's silver Cuban link jumped through my mind after asking his question.

"Do we gotta do this the hard way, or will we be easy and try to work together? After all, this is Joe Boy's second time meeting you like this, and I'm not trying to miss the money on this round like we did on Christmas two decades ago."

The name Joe Boy crawled up my veins. When I looked in the mirror that sat behind the handicapped killer, I watched his eyes slant evilly, forcing his bushy unibrow to rise. That's when I saw it in him. Even after so long, I could still feel his demonic facial expression hawking down on me that dreadful day. The only thing that was different was his grey beard and tricking appearance, but he was damn sho' the man causing the nightmare that I never was able to get rid of. At that second, I knew whatever was about to happen wasn't gonna end well for me.

Chris Green

150

Chapter 17
Kay-Kay

The sun had dropped quickly by the time I made it across town from Buckhead to the south side. I had called Melly at least ten times since then and still hadn't succeeded in reaching him. My curiosity was eating at me, and I had yet to stop thinking about the number I ran across in the back of his cell. Knowing that I was too weak to handle pressure with finding out shit, I texted the bitch's number, acting just like him as we rode down the street.

"So, why did you want me to text you?" I messaged the phone.

Within less than a minute, there was a reply coming through.

"You have a hard time picking up the phone to follow directions. You need to get out of that house. Please listen. You're in danger of being caught."

My mind wondered what the hell this bitch meant by getting caught, so I kept digging.

"Get caught for what? Explain to me what you mean."

Just like the first message, the next zoomed in immediately.

"The house you're sitting in, Sal has you there, and he's trying to kill you. Joe Boy is gonna try and murder you if you're not out of there in time. If you can get to the garage, there is a gun under the green toolbox. Grab it if you're in need of protection. Please get out!"

My stomach turned in knots when I read the text, and whoever was giving the info damn sure didn't sound like they were joking.

My dad drove me all the way to the exact location. When we reached the street, I requested for him to park a few doors down. Even though he hated rules, he obliged, allowing me to step out of the car on the empty sidewalk. I could see Melly's Durango sitting in the parking lot, and I prayed that he didn't have a bitch sleeping inside it.

Holding my purse tight, I pulled the phone out, trailing up the side of the garage. The numbers 6-2-6 sat on the wooden edge rail, and that shit bubbled my guts even more. Sneaking up to the first window I spotted, I peeked through.

Melly was tied up in a chair with someone standing behind him. I could see a person sitting in a wheelchair posted in front of them but couldn't make out a face. Using my phone, I pressed record, placing a hand over my mouth. These bitches had my baby tied up, and I wasn't about to sit back and just watch them hurt him. Getting what I need on film, I texted my father and asked could he call the police for backup while I took my chances on going in.

Creeping up along the home, I turned the doorknob handle to the garage and was surprised when it opened. Observing my surroundings, I moved slowly inside. It took me a while, but tiptoeing around the small four-wall room, I ended up running right into the giant green toolbox. Reaching my hand underneath, I grabbed the .380 pistol and made my way for the entrance to the home.

* * *

Melly

"See, Melly. That bracelet is worth at least $1.1 million, and come to find out, and there was eight of 'em made. Now, of course, I got the first six," He flashed the pieces in his hand. "But the last two seem to be a problem. You wouldn't want to die like this, would you? All for a mistake?" He rotated his head, trying to pick with my brain.

"Nah, but I would rather die before a nigga like you win. I ain't got shit for you."

The nigga started giggling like I was a fucking comedian. Pointing a finger to my face, he scowled. "You are one ungrateful bitch. I'm gonna have Joe Boy cut your head off just like I did your dad, except yours will be my trophy."

My vision happened to rotate back to the mirror, and I saw Kay-Kay creeping through the back door, sending a chill down my back. She was carrying a gun, and I nearly cried, wondering how in the fuck she found me. I couldn't allow her to get hurt. I had to make a move. Just as I saw Sal's sight move behind us. I jumped from my chair, rushing over to him. I crashed my entire body into the seat, sending us both to the ground. The shotgun flung across the floor as he tried to wrestle me down while the rope was tied on my hands. Joe Boy started to move towards us, and a loud gunshot froze the entire room.

Bang!

Rolling my head around to make sure Kay-Kay was safe, I watched as Joe Boy crumbled to the ground, face first. Moving over towards me, she placed the gun to Sal's face.

"I'll kill you before you take us, now bet on that!"

Placing his hands flat out on the floor, Kay-Kay helped me untie the restraints so I could get up. I wasted no time snatching up the six bracelets lying on the floorboard. Kicking Sal in the face, he grunted distastefully.

Taking the gun from my girl, I was about to pull the trigger and felt her hand grab ahold of mines.

"No, Melly, you can't. If you do, I'll never be able to save you from this. We need to call the police. Now," she suggested with her hands shaking.

"Kay-Kay, we can't. You'll probably be sent home while I'm on the way to a prison cell, and I'm not leaving you. We gotta go." I tried to grab her hand and leave.

"Her tight grip forced me to stop again. I saw the tears that were ready to drop from her eyes as she spoke.

"Melly, if you don't listen to me now, there will be no future. It won't be a second chance, baby. You have to trust me now and have faith that I'm right. Call the cops, baby. We are gonna beat this together. If we run, we might as well just run forever. Please!" she begged, holding on to my shirt.

I knew for a fact that I was about to take a long ride if I was caught on that scene. Nothing would be able to save me in the courts, and all I had left to fight for was Kayona. No matter how bad I didn't want to, I had to trust her word. Hearing sirens near towards the home, I nodded, placing a kiss on her lips. Grabbing her hand, we walked out the front foot together as the patrol cars started to slide into the yard.

Kay-Kay's parents were coming across the street in a panic, and officers started to flood from the vehicles, heading inside. A couple of rookie officers quickly placed me into cuffs, and that's when Detective Solomon's head rose out of his Ram truck. He was dressed in an all-black suit and a pair of brown Steve Madden's.

"I guess you're gonna be able to explain what happened here tonight, right?" He looked at Kay-Kay and me seriously.

"I was kidnapped. I had no choice."

He kept his lips sealed for a second, just starting to see if my story would switch. After holding my grounds, he nodded to another suited officer that walked calmly over to me. "Mr. Hicks, you're under arrest for the murder of Denaisha Spencer. You have the right to remain silent. Anything you say can be used against you in the court of law."

"Wait, he ain't do that. It's a mistake!" Kay-Kay yelled in disappointment.

Solomon gave her a pathetic look. "I'm sorry, young lady. He has to be taken in. I can clear this up as self-defense if everything points out to be what he says, but I can't help you with the child issue. You gotta face a judge. I'm sorry." He pulled me towards his truck.

"Melly, I promise, baby. I'll bring you home, ya hear me? Don't give up on me," Kay-Kay cried her eyes out.

My father-in-law, Mr. Benjamin, came and hugged my neck. "Don't worry about it, Meltavious. Don't say anything. I'll have my lawyer down to see you tonight, son."

"Thanks, Mr. Wilcox."

Looking back at Kaycake, I blew her a kiss. "I trust you, bay. You said I believe, and I do. Get me back home to you," I pleaded with pain eating me alive.

"I will. Trust me. Trust me." She formed a heart with her fingers as Detective Solomon placed me in the backseat.

As I drove leaving my Queen in the street, watching me be hauled away, I learned the value of two things, Family and the woman who says she has your back. Now that I was aware of what I had by my side, I had to fight in order to not lose that forever, and I was done with all the rest. In my heart, I just prayed that little Denaisha could find it in her spirit to forgive me.

Chapter 18
Kay-Kay

It had been almost seven months since Melly had been incarcerated, and it was dragging the shit out of me. Bleeko ended up snitching and trying to take the stand, but was released on a hundred-thousand-dollar bond. Leaving Melly in jail alone to be placed as the murderer. Two days after his arrest, I was called down to his cousin, Nita's, house about an incident nobody wanted to speak on. By the time I reached her street, I had noticed that her apartment building was going up in flames. I got out of the car staring at the horror until a hand tapped my shoulder. Turning around, I locked eyes with Dunk. He held Nina's baby in his arms, heartbroken at the sight. I could see from the wet face he was trying to clear up that Nina didn't make it out alive.

"She wanted me to make sure you took her little one. She said that she couldn't live without Melly, and it was time to give up. I walked to the store and came back. She sat the baby outside and turned the house up in flames," he explained, placing little Maliyah into my arms.

"Please tell me this isn't true?" I asked him with a dreadful expression. I knew that the news would kill Melly, and I didn't want to give the story after he was already facing so many obstacles.

"Thank you, Dunk. You know that she means a lot to Melly," I gave my appreciation to the utmost.

"It's all I can do. Silent Avenue is home. Nina was like big sis. Give Melly my condolences."

"I will."

I sat back holding Maliyah as if she were my own while watching the bright red thirty-foot flames blaring from her window. The will to give away life, seeds, sanity, and the blessing to worship your loved ones that took a lost soul.

Through the crowd, I watched Cat appear with a kitten stuffed in his coat pocket. He was dressed in a pair of khakis and an old Bill Cosby Coogi sweater. He came a posted directly beside me, with a down face. "I told Melly that I never liked Joe Boy. Franklin was always meant to win. They lost regardless of him being gone, Kay-Kay," he said with wide eyes.

"Cat, what are you talking about? It seems like everyone lost to me. They're all gone and still leaving by the day. It doesn't feel good at all." I started to rock Maliyah, who was now crying.

Watching him dig into his shirt, he reached around his neck and pulled off a silver bracelet. Placing it in my hand, he smiled. "Just take this and think of Melly when you feel down. Franklin gave it to me a long time ago. I knew that I would find a place for it to be. It's made me smile for some decades, so I know it can do the same for you." He grinned ear to ear while cuddling the cat in his jacket.

My face lit up with excitement after noticing what I had. Melly explained to me the other night over the phone about the conversation with Sal, and according to the eight bracelets I had in my possession, I was about to surprise the fucking world. I had to go to the bank immediately and check in with the manager that was over the funds. Once he approved me and I had access, I was gonna show these bitches why my name was Kayona Wilcox.

Heading for the car, I climbed behind the wheel, strapping the little one in with me. I didn't have a car seat, and my driving was better than good. My main focus was to get her to safety.

Starting the engine, I left out of the crowded lot and was able to slide through the ambulance and fire trucks easily. Little mama was so cute and relaxed in my hand. She showed me the blessings of being a baby. Me taking this step would bless us both. If it took for me to step in to make stuff better for her, then it was just gonna be us 'til the end. My next step was simple. Head down Rice Street, Fulton County Jail, and see Melly. It was time to see if I could make a few things change. Even though we spoke daily, and he was straight on his commissary, it didn't draw me closer to my other half. I needed him home.

Chapter 19
Melly

I was more than frustrated and rolling through Fulton was an all-out drag session. I had a paid attorney but barely got my proper visits. Now the court was trying to pin the murder of little Denaisha if Bleeko agreed to testify on me. The sad thing about it was that the streets claimed he was planning on really going through with it. After these long months, I craved my woman, and I missed the freedom that I once was able to control. Now that I was experiencing some of the nastiest times, it was showing the reality of how bad shit could really get.

Hearing my door sound off, it slid open.

"Hicks, you got an attorney visit," I heard the officer announce through the speaker.

Grabbing a pen and paper with a few legal pages, I headed out to the visitation area in 700 and pulled those same raggedy-ass metal stairs to my booth.

Getting inside, it was empty. I waited for a moment, a moment too long that was about to make me say fuck it. I just know that school is damn sho important. I never ended up converting to Muslim after what happened with Joe Boy, but I still read the Quran. In the end, it seemed like he got the bad end of the sticky bush. My girl got a body under her belt, and that shit was justified. We beat that shit within two months of my bid and had been stuck on the second case ever since. Things were looking shaky, but a speedy trial is what I was heading for, and that would determine whether I walked out the door or not.

My whole train of thoughts went out of the window when I looked up at Detective Solomon walking inside of my attorney booth.

"How you doing, Mr. Hicks?" He leaned against the door frame as If he didn't have a care in the universe.

"How am I? I'm facing a life sentence for a murder that I'm not trying to accept. I have a whole life ahead of me. I wasn't meant to be caught up in any of this. I was only defending myself," I stressed through clenched jaws.

"And I've heard that numerous of times before Hicks. Now I know usually I would sit here and baptize you in a bucket of misery about how you screwed up, and I warned you. Instead, I'll just pass with saying I do believe you no matter how bad I despise your choice of friends. Me and your father weren't the closest of brothers, but he stuck his neck out for me, so I'll give you a favor back on the head. Stay up, and you'll be out of here soon. Depending on if you can handle your talkative Silent Avenue homie. I'll leave that up to you." He slid the slick comment in as if I didn't know he wanted his foster brother dead, just as bad as me. I had a game to win and squealing to this punk-ass oink puppy baby wasn't involved in it. Just as he came, he left, and I was heading back to the dorm with a heavy decision on my mind. I had the paperwork with Bleeko's government snitching on me. He was out hiding, spending money like I wasn't sitting in this hellhole banged up. The fool never even tried to contact me. All I could do was wait like the pig told me to and prepare for trial because I wasn't taking shit. If that meant Bleeko's face for my freedom, then I was gonna prove that I was a bigger dawg. One call was all it took.

* * *

Six Days Later
Avon Avenue
Bleeko

I had just finished stroking this new lil cutty from the back when a move hit my line. I needed a spare and oil change, so it was definitely worth my while. Pulling in, I jammed the doobie into the ashtray, glancing around for the money-green Acura truck. Once I spotted it, I turned in next to his car.

The tinted windows were rattling from the Boosie CD that was thumping on the speakers. I waved to get the nigga's attention and watched the window roll down. Dunk was sitting in the front seat with a fully loaded semi. His look alone said what he was there for, and before I could muster a move, he let off four rapid shots.

Plak! Plak! Plak! Plak!

Two struck me hard. One in the cheek, another in the hand when I tried to block the hollow tip, but the other slugs shattered both side windows.

Dunk and six more shooters stepped out and personally walked over to my car. Blood was pouring from my face and hand, and my foot was stuck trying to mash the whip in reverse.

"You didn't stay loyal to the hood, so the block ain't staying Silent with you," he spat, aiming his gun at me. The rest of his killers did the same, and the last thing I remember was me cursing that bitch-ass nigga, Solomon, to die before numerous guns started to sound off at one time. I never felt the last breath leave me as the sound of metal being riddled off filled the air.

Chris Green

Chapter 20
Melly
Fulton County Jail
Three Months Later
August 18, 2020

Watching the woman cut the ID band off my wrist, I walked through the exit doors with my head held high. It turns out that Bleeko's fingerprints showed up on the gun that killed little Denaisha. His testimony was never useful after they had to peel him from the car that he got plastered to. The great part about it was my trial was not only did I have a good case, but the mother came and testified on my behalf that I wasn't her daughter's killer. Her statement alone freed me and got me a civil lawsuit win from the state. Kay-Kay's video of Sal and Joe Boy holding me hostage got the case of 626 Street thrown out, per the judge. It was a scary feeling fighting for your life, and the people had the decision to hang the rope around your throat before they kicked you.

Smelling the free air when I walked out of 901 doors, I turned my head and spotted my baby posted like a light bulb. Her tummy was nearly about to pop due to my last days of being a monster at home. I now had custody of my baby cousin, Maliyah. She was like my own, and it would always give my daughter, Fall, a chance to be raised around our bloodline. Kay-Kay was dressed in a white Gucci sundress and pair of Louie pumps. Her makeup was dabbed up perfectly, and her red skin was shining like buttered toast.

Moving over to her, I sucked on her bottom lip and grabbed a handful of ass. It was soft like tissue, and I knew for a fact that some ass eating was surely going on tonight.

"Hey, my Queen. I missed you." I grinned, playing through her hair, and running my tongue across her neck, The smell of cotton candy extract was blowing from her body, and nothing but her bare flesh was worn under the fabric. I could tell when I pulled her in for a hug.

"I missed you too, Melly. It's been long enough, baby, but it's been worth it. I told you to trust me, so are you happy with how things ended?" she asked me with her dimples poking out like a sore thumb.

Looking around the sky for a second, I gazed back at the bullshitting prison and shook my head. "Baby, I'm satisfied with anything you tell me from now on. Just having and knowing that we share a bond with our visions makes me smile and appreciate life much more. After all, you visioned it all." I grinned, rubbing her huge stomach.

Digging in her bra, she pulled out a set of keys, cheesing all hard.

"What do those keys lead to?" I grabbed Maliyah up in my hands, blushing at how thick and prissy my baby looked at that second. It was nothing that was gonna stop me from sucking her little pearl boat and running two of my fingers in my pussy to see how sloppy it got for me. A year had a nigga's hormones raging, and I was happy to see some titties and hair instead of hard legs and basketball.

"It leads to our new start in Denver, Colorado. It's ready for you. I know how much you said that *X Games* was your favorite. Now we can be right down the street from the Kicks that you like to spend your time watching and doing Melly. My graduation was last month, and it was amazing. And even though you didn't get a chance to make it, I dedicated it all to you. I reached our goal, and it's all because of you." She got inside the car after I strapped Maliyah in her chair.

"No, Kaycake. You're my light and the reason why I'm pushing to be the best man I can be. You make me complete, and I guess our dreams were telling us something way back.

It was explaining that we were meant to be, and I'm willing to sacrifice anything to have you by my side because I know you will do the same.

"Awww, thanks, Melly Welly." She pinched my cheek. "I'm always here for you. That's what I'm here for," she added before leaning over dropping the eight bracelets in my lap. My face dropped in awe as I looked back up at her bright smile.

"Before you say anything, we're leaving tomorrow. What all do you have to settle before we depart? I know this city means a lot to you?"

I pondered on a few things first before I gave her directions to where we needed to stop first. Typing the address into GPS, I was sliding down in front of the home within twenty-five minutes. It looked the same, besides the few new model cars sitting out front. I didn't know If my plan would work, but it was surely worth a try.

Climbing out of the car, Kay-Kay stayed in the driver's seat, allowing me to handle my affairs alone. Getting to the front door, I knocked three times and stepped back.

It didn't take but a few seconds before I heard the door opening, and she appeared from the folds of her foyer, looking prettier than ever. She was dressed in all black tights and fitted shirt to start her normal workout, her pearly thirty-twos were showing, and she couldn't help but hug me once the screen door broke our separation.

"Hi, stranger. I'm glad to see that you made it out. You deserved it."

"Thanks, ma." I toyed with my hands, knowing this was a bad chick standing in front of me. I had to come to show my gratefulness for her assistance and compensate her. Pulling the white envelope from my back pocket, I handed it to her. "This is for you. It's thirty thousand dollars. I just wanna say much love for all your support. I can call you a true friend. I don't have too many of those." I chuckled, trying to be smooth but thirsty at the same time.

"I think that you are a great friend Melly. I'll always be here if you need me, and you don't have to call to stop by. You're always welcome." She leaned in, pecking my lips.

The shit shocked me, and I didn't even have time to react quick enough. I knew for a fact Kay-Kay witnessed that, and I wasn't gonna be surprised if she was about to spring out of the damn car at any second with a giant hunting knife and burning chain like the *Ghost Rider*. Instead of being nervous and feeling guilty, I blushed.

"Always Jemora. My info is inside. Please don't hesitate to call me if you need me." I turned, walking down the steps. As I trailed back to the car, I got in and cut my eyes to wifey. Her gorgeous, mesmerizing pupils studied me, but her grin said that she clearly wasn't mad.

"I like her. She's hot," Kay-Kay snickered, driving off while I waved goodbye. "Does she kiss good?"

"Not like you." I smooched her juicy pink lips. "One more stop, baby, and we can slide out of here for good," I mentioned, thinking about the memories I was preparing to leave behind.

It took nearly thirty minutes to reach the west side, but the sun was just setting when I crossed the zone one city limits. Driving down Silent Avenue. I thought about all the shit I tried and got away with. The non-sense I forced into my life that could have easily been avoided. It was all in vain.

Slowing down when I reached the Tasty Dog Restaurant, I viewed his ass and slid right over to the curb, rolling down the window.

"Yo Cat...Uncle Cat. I called out to him as he rested under the roofing shade patio. Four of his kittens danced around his leg while he held up a pack of Mackerel. Looking up at me, he squinted his eyes as if he just saw a Phantom.

"Melly? Is that you, nephew?"

"Yes. Now come on. We out this bitch." I waved him over to the car.

"Ohhhh shit, y'all. I told you we were gone make it. Come on, Sprinkles. Let's go." He picked up three cats as the other followed. Jumping in the backseat with his adorable sidekicks, he leaned over the seat at Kay-Kay and me smiling.

"So, where we going y'all? Is it filled with tuna and milk?"

"We're headed to Colorado, Unc. You can have all the tuna and milk you want, my nigga." I laughed before pulling off.

Chris Green

Chapter 21
Denver, Colorado
Suburban Townhomes
Four Weeks Later
X Games Competition
Melly

The show was more than amazing, and it was magnificent. Unlike anything I ever witnessed out of my entire life, I never knew that I would be sharing my dream with the woman I fell in love with in junior high. Our baby girl, Fall Hicks, was eight pounds and two ounces with hazel peepers, just like her mother. Since we made it to Colorado, Kaycake and I had opened six different businesses. Two funeral homes, a few laundromats, and our own Vision Reading Establishment to practice our newly discovered gift. It seems that our dreams were more in common than we thought, and somehow, we were able to feel one another's energy. I knew that we truly were one when she took the risk of her own life for me. Now nine million dollars later, my three babies were doing more than well. Uncle Cat had his own spot, breeding kittens, and he was actually making a fortune from the shit. Who would have ever known? Bleeko had a nasty funeral. Word on the street was that a black-tinted van came through and let the whole clip go on all his fam. The treachery of snitching when you were raised on Silent Avenue was like a curse being placed on someone who desired to be possessed by a demon.

"Baby, remember the time. We still have to meet with Mr. Beasley at three. This is an important client, and we can bank on a franchise if we close this deal," she explained as Maliyah chewed on a soft, warm pretzel.

I held Fall and couldn't believe that I had my own princess to raise for the world now. Kay-Kay literally called out our entire life since ninth grade, and it fell accordingly. We had money, each other, a new family, and the nightmares felt like they were actually over.

Hearing my phone ring, I shuffled through my coat pocket until I reached it, answering the Georgia area code number. I placed it to my ear.

"Yo, what's good?

"Melly, I think we need to talk," a deep but smooth voice spoke like shit was all bad.

"What? Who the hell is this?"

"I need to get the entire story of what happened to Mama June and your father on the table. I want my half of what's owed to me, and I think you have it. I'll give you the choice. Sack up half of the cash and ship it to my designated address. If not, the nightmares are gonna begin again, Meltavious. You don't have to beg family for love over here. You're loved." He chuckled evilly into my ear.

The dial tone ending forced a lump into my throat. The mysterious call was one that didn't sound too good, but too accurate not to believe. Just as I thought we were finally at peace, the nightmare was starting over.

To Be Continued...
Nightmare on Silent Avenue 2: Breaking Dawn
Coming Soon

Submission Guideline

Submit the first three chapters of your completed manuscript to ldpsubmissions@gmail.com, subject line: Your book's title. The manuscript must be in a .doc file and sent as an attachment. Document should be in Times New Roman, double spaced and in size 12 font. Also, provide your synopsis and full contact information. If sending multiple submissions, they must each be in a separate email.

Have a story but no way to send it electronically? You can still submit to LDP/Ca$h Presents. Send in the first three chapters, written or typed, of your completed manuscript to:

LDP: Submissions Dept
Po Box 944
Stockbridge, Ga 30281

DO NOT send original manuscript. Must be a duplicate.

Provide your synopsis and a cover letter containing your full contact information.

Thanks for considering LDP and Ca$h Presents.

<u>NEW RELEASE</u>

FRIEND OR FOE 3 by MIMI
A GANGSTA'S KARMA by FLAME
NIGHTMARE ON SILENT AVE by CHRIS
GREEN

BLOOD OF A BOSS **VI**

SHADOWS OF THE GAME II

TRAP BASTARD II

By **Askari**

LOYAL TO THE GAME **IV**

By **T.J. & Jelissa**

IF TRUE SAVAGE **VIII**

MIDNIGHT CARTEL IV

DOPE BOY MAGIC IV

CITY OF KINGZ III

NIGHTMARE ON SILENT AVE II

By **Chris Green**

BLAST FOR ME **III**

A SAVAGE DOPEBOY III

CUTTHROAT MAFIA III

DUFFLE BAG CARTEL VII

HEARTLESS GOON VI

By **Ghost**

A HUSTLER'S DECEIT III

KILL ZONE II

BAE BELONGS TO ME III

A DOPE BOY'S QUEEN III

By **Aryanna**

COKE KINGS V

KING OF THE TRAP III

By **T.J. Edwards**

Chris Green

GORILLAZ IN THE BAY V

3X KRAZY III

De'Kari

KINGPIN KILLAZ IV

STREET KINGS III

PAID IN BLOOD III

CARTEL KILLAZ IV

DOPE GODS III

Hood Rich

SINS OF A HUSTLA II

ASAD

RICH $AVAGE II

By Troublesome

YAYO V

Bred In The Game 2

S. Allen

CREAM III

By Yolanda Moore

SON OF A DOPE FIEND III

HEAVEN GOT A GHETTO II

By Renta

LOYALTY AIN'T PROMISED III

By Keith Williams

I'M NOTHING WITHOUT HIS LOVE II

SINS OF A THUG II

TO THE THUG I LOVED BEFORE II

By Monet Dragun

QUIET MONEY IV

EXTENDED CLIP III

THUG LIFE IV

By **Trai'Quan**

THE STREETS MADE ME III

By **Larry D. Wright**

IF YOU CROSS ME ONCE II

By **Anthony Fields**

THE STREETS WILL NEVER CLOSE II

By **K'ajji**

HARD AND RUTHLESS III

Von Diesel

KILLA KOUNTY II

By Khufu

MOBBED UP III

By King Rio

MONEY GAME II

By Smoove Dolla

A GANGSTA'S KARMA II

By FLAME

Available Now

RESTRAINING ORDER **I & II**

By **CA$H & Coffee**

LOVE KNOWS NO BOUNDARIES **I II & III**

By **Coffee**

RAISED AS A GOON I, II, III & IV

BRED BY THE SLUMS I, II, III

BLAST FOR ME I & II

ROTTEN TO THE CORE I II III

A BRONX TALE I, II, III

DUFFLE BAG CARTEL I II III IV V VI

HEARTLESS GOON I II III IV V

A SAVAGE DOPEBOY I II

DRUG LORDS I II III

CUTTHROAT MAFIA I II

KING OF THE TRENCHES

By **Ghost**

LAY IT DOWN **I & II**

LAST OF A DYING BREED I II

BLOOD STAINS OF A SHOTTA I & II III

By **Jamaica**

LOYAL TO THE GAME I II III

LIFE OF SIN I, II III

By **TJ & Jelissa**

BLOODY COMMAS I & II

SKI MASK CARTEL I II & III

KING OF NEW YORK I II,III IV V

RISE TO POWER I II III

COKE KINGS I II III IV

BORN HEARTLESS I II III IV

KING OF THE TRAP I II

By **T.J. Edwards**

Nightmare on Silent Avenue

IF LOVING HIM IS WRONG…I & II

LOVE ME EVEN WHEN IT HURTS I II III

By **Jelissa**

WHEN THE STREETS CLAP BACK I & II III

THE HEART OF A SAVAGE I II III

By **Jibril Williams**

A DISTINGUISHED THUG STOLE MY HEART I II & III

LOVE SHOULDN'T HURT I II III IV

RENEGADE BOYS I II III IV

PAID IN KARMA I II III

SAVAGE STORMS I II

AN UNFORESEEN LOVE

By **Meesha**

A GANGSTER'S CODE I &, II III

A GANGSTER'S SYN I II III

THE SAVAGE LIFE I II III

CHAINED TO THE STREETS I II III

BLOOD ON THE MONEY I II III

By **J-Blunt**

PUSH IT TO THE LIMIT

By **Bre' Hayes**

BLOOD OF A BOSS **I, II, III, IV, V**

SHADOWS OF THE GAME

TRAP BASTARD

By **Askari**

THE STREETS BLEED MURDER **I, II & III**

THE HEART OF A GANGSTA I II& III

By **Jerry Jackson**

CUM FOR ME I II III IV V VI VII

An **LDP Erotica Collaboration**

BRIDE OF A HUSTLA **I II & II**

THE FETTI GIRLS **I, II& III**

CORRUPTED BY A GANGSTA I, II III, IV

BLINDED BY HIS LOVE

THE PRICE YOU PAY FOR LOVE I, II ,III

DOPE GIRL MAGIC I II III

By **Destiny Skai**

WHEN A GOOD GIRL GOES BAD

By **Adrienne**

THE COST OF LOYALTY I II III

By Kweli

A GANGSTER'S REVENGE **I II III & IV**

THE BOSS MAN'S DAUGHTERS I II III IV V

A SAVAGE LOVE **I & II**

BAE BELONGS TO ME I II

A HUSTLER'S DECEIT I, II, III

WHAT BAD BITCHES DO I, II, III

SOUL OF A MONSTER I II III

KILL ZONE

A DOPE BOY'S QUEEN I II

By **Aryanna**

A KINGPIN'S AMBITON

A KINGPIN'S AMBITION **II**

I MURDER FOR THE DOUGH

Nightmare on Silent Avenue

By **Ambitious**

TRUE SAVAGE I II III IV V VI VII

DOPE BOY MAGIC I, II, III

MIDNIGHT CARTEL I II III

CITY OF KINGZ I II

NIGHTMARE ON SILENT AVE

By **Chris Green**

A DOPEBOY'S PRAYER

By **Eddie "Wolf" Lee**

THE KING CARTEL **I, II & III**

By **Frank Gresham**

THESE NIGGAS AIN'T LOYAL **I, II & III**

By **Nikki Tee**

GANGSTA SHYT **I II &III**

By **CATO**

THE ULTIMATE BETRAYAL

By **Phoenix**

BOSS'N UP **I , II & III**

By **Royal Nicole**

I LOVE YOU TO DEATH

By **Destiny J**

I RIDE FOR MY HITTA

I STILL RIDE FOR MY HITTA

By **Misty Holt**

LOVE & CHASIN' PAPER

By **Qay Crockett**

TO DIE IN VAIN

SINS OF A HUSTLA

By **ASAD**

BROOKLYN HUSTLAZ

By **Boogsy Morina**

BROOKLYN ON LOCK I & II

By **Sonovia**

GANGSTA CITY

By **Teddy Duke**

A DRUG KING AND HIS DIAMOND I & II III

A DOPEMAN'S RICHES

HER MAN, MINE'S TOO I, II

CASH MONEY HO'S

THE WIFEY I USED TO BE I II

By Nicole Goosby

TRAPHOUSE KING **I II & III**

KINGPIN KILLAZ I II III

STREET KINGS I II

PAID IN BLOOD **I II**

CARTEL KILLAZ I II III

DOPE GODS I II

By **Hood Rich**

LIPSTICK KILLAH **I, II, III**

CRIME OF PASSION I II & III

FRIEND OR FOE I II III

By **Mimi**

STEADY MOBBN' **I, II, III**

THE STREETS STAINED MY SOUL I II

Nightmare on Silent Avenue

By **Marcellus Allen**
WHO SHOT YA **I, II, III**
SON OF A DOPE FIEND I II
HEAVEN GOT A GHETTO
Renta
GORILLAZ IN THE BAY **I II III IV**
TEARS OF A GANGSTA I II
3X KRAZY I II
DE'KARI
TRIGGADALE I II III
Elijah R. Freeman
GOD BLESS THE TRAPPERS I, II, III
THESE SCANDALOUS STREETS I, II, III
FEAR MY GANGSTA I, II, III IV, V
THESE STREETS DON'T LOVE NOBODY I, II
BURY ME A G I, II, III, IV, V
A GANGSTA'S EMPIRE I, II, III, IV
THE DOPEMAN'S BODYGAURD I II
THE REALEST KILLAZ I II III
THE LAST OF THE OGS I II III
Tranay Adams
THE STREETS ARE CALLING
Duquie Wilson
MARRIED TO A BOSS I II III
By Destiny Skai & Chris Green
KINGZ OF THE GAME I II III IV V
Playa Ray

183

Chris Green

SLAUGHTER GANG I II III

RUTHLESS HEART I II III

By Willie Slaughter

FUK SHYT

By Blakk Diamond

DON'T F#CK WITH MY HEART I II

By Linnea

ADDICTED TO THE DRAMA I II III

IN THE ARM OF HIS BOSS II

By Jamila

YAYO I II III IV

A SHOOTER'S AMBITION I II

BRED IN THE GAME

By S. Allen

TRAP GOD I II III

RICH $AVAGE

By Troublesome

FOREVER GANGSTA

GLOCKS ON SATIN SHEETS I II

By Adrian Dulan

TOE TAGZ I II III

LEVELS TO THIS SHYT I II

By Ah'Million

KINGPIN DREAMS I II III

By Paper Boi Rari

CONFESSIONS OF A GANGSTA I II III

By Nicholas Lock

Nightmare on Silent Avenue

I'M NOTHING WITHOUT HIS LOVE

SINS OF A THUG

TO THE THUG I LOVED BEFORE

By Monet Dragun

CAUGHT UP IN THE LIFE I II III

By Robert Baptiste

NEW TO THE GAME I II III

MONEY, MURDER & MEMORIES I II III

By **Malik D. Rice**

LIFE OF A SAVAGE I II III

A GANGSTA'S QUR'AN I II III

MURDA SEASON I II III

GANGLAND CARTEL I II III

CHI'RAQ GANGSTAS I II III

KILLERS ON ELM STREET I II III

JACK BOYZ N DA BRONX I II III

A DOPEBOY'S DREAM

By **Romell Tukes**

LOYALTY AIN'T PROMISED I II

By Keith Williams

QUIET MONEY I II III

THUG LIFE I II III

EXTENDED CLIP I II

By **Trai'Quan**

THE STREETS MADE ME I II

By **Larry D. Wright**

THE ULTIMATE SACRIFICE I, II, III, IV, V, VI

KHADIFI

IF YOU CROSS ME ONCE

ANGEL I II

IN THE BLINK OF AN EYE

By **Anthony Fields**

THE LIFE OF A HOOD STAR

By Ca$h & Rashia Wilson

THE STREETS WILL NEVER CLOSE

By K'ajji

CREAM I II

By Yolanda Moore

NIGHTMARES OF A HUSTLA I II III

By King Dream

CONCRETE KILLA I II

By Kingpen

HARD AND RUTHLESS I II

MOB TOWN 251

By Von Diesel

GHOST MOB

Stilloan Robinson

MOB TIES I II

By SayNoMore

BODYMORE MURDERLAND I II III

By Delmont Player

FOR THE LOVE OF A BOSS

By C. D. Blue

MOBBED UP I II

By King Rio

KILLA KOUNTY

By Khufu

MONEY GAME

By Smoove Dolla

A GANGSTA'S KARMA

By FLAME

<u>BOOKS BY LDP'S CEO, CA$H</u>

<u>TRUST IN NO MAN</u>

<u>TRUST IN NO MAN 2</u>

<u>TRUST IN NO MAN 3</u>

<u>BONDED BY BLOOD</u>

<u>SHORTY GOT A THUG</u>

<u>THUGS CRY</u>

<u>THUGS CRY 2</u>

<u>THUGS CRY 3</u>

<u>TRUST NO BITCH</u>

<u>TRUST NO BITCH 2</u>

<u>TRUST NO BITCH 3</u>

<u>TIL MY CASKET DROPS</u>

<u>RESTRAINING ORDER</u>

<u>RESTRAINING ORDER 2</u>

<u>IN LOVE WITH A CONVICT</u>

<u>LIFE OF A HOOD STAR</u>

Nightmare on Silent Avenue

www.ingramcontent.com/pod-product-compliance
Lightning Source LLC
Chambersburg PA
CBHW070518260626
47161CB00004B/1580